When You Speak
My Name

Tish Cook
_2011_

Tish Cook

Sweet Prairie Publishing

Sweet Prairie Publishing

9523 Wandering Trails Lane

Dawson, Ill. 62520-3111

Library of Congress Number: 2010925254

ISBN 978-1-4507-1024-4

Front and back covers designed by Dale Lael

Printed in the United States of America

Author's Note

This story is fiction, but based on a few facts I discovered while I was working on my family tree.

My great grandmother, Victoria Yoakum, was born in southern Missouri in 1852. Her mother was Cherokee Indian and her father was a white man (my mother always told me that Victoria's father was French Canadian, but I can't confirm that). Victoria spent most of her early childhood in Missouri, but by the time she was 12 she was an orphan. I don't know how her mother died, but I have documentation that her father was murdered in 1864 in Oregon county Missouri. His killer was subsequently caught, tried and hung for the crime.

Victoria then traveled to Menard county Illinois and lived the remainder of her life in and around the town of Athens, Illinois. She died in 1936 and is buried somewhere in the old West Cemetery in Athens, but I'm unable to find her headstone.

Once I discovered these facts, it was like Victoria's spirit was nearby and saying to me "There's a story here. Write it." Her amazing life and the Cherokee Indian belief in the Spirit World has inspired me to do just that.

The format of the story – called "parallel timelines" – is unique. Alternating chapters will take you into both the 19th and 21st centuries as you follow the lives of Victoria and her great granddaughter, Julie. I've even added a few French and Cherokee words for flavor.

Characters Victoria, Henri and Amy Levalier and Rogers Yochem are based on my maternal ancestors. All other characters are fictitious and any resemblance to actual persons, living or dead is purely coincidental.

In loving memory of

Willetta Mortimer

and

Felicia Cook

I will speak your names often.

When you speak the name of someone
who has passed away, their
spirit will draw near to you.

~ Old wives tale ~

Chapter 1

September 09, 1852
Oregon County, Missouri

He gently stroked the infant's tiny arm with his calloused finger. "*Elle est parfaite,* she's perfect." His voice quivered. "She has your eyes."

Amy glanced down at the tiny bundle. "But your nose."

He kissed her softly. "I love you."

"And I you."

They stood on the banks of the babbling stream and waited for the ceremony to begin. The air was cool and fresh; the scent of wet stones hung over them like a blanket. Catey had witnessed many naming ceremonies before, but with no village chief or elder present, she would conduct this one. She looked at Amy and nodded solemnly. Amy handed her the infant, then sat down on a nearby rock. Henri stood close to his wife, his hand on her shoulder. She was still weak from the long and difficult labor.

Catey sloshed into the stream, found a shallow spot where the water had been warmed by the late summer sun and held the naked child out for all to see.

Her powerful voice filled the morning air. "Oh Great Creator, look down and see this Cherokee child, this *a-yo-tli*. Her mother, Little Sparrow and her father, Henri wish to name her. They say the child's eyes are the color of the sacred eagle, and she will be called Eagle Eyes. We ask that you give Eagle Eyes a long and happy life."

Catey placed her hand over the child's mouth and nose and gently immersed her in the swishing pool seven times. The startled child twitched each time her tiny body touched the frothy water, but she didn't cry out. The medicine woman looked down at the squirming infant. Her instincts told her this child would be special.

Catey motioned to Henri, who walked quickly into the stream. He wrapped the quivering infant in a large, colorful cotton blanket, smiled at Catey, then waded back to Amy and handed the child to her.

Francois looked at the proud parents and said, "I like it. It is a good name, Eagle Eyes."

"She'll also have an English name," Amy said rocking the shivering child.

Henri nodded. "We have decided to call her Victoria."

"For the queen?" Francois asked.

"*Oui,*" Henri replied. His mind stepped back to their parents, who still lived in Canada.

Francois seemed to read his brother's thoughts. "I wish they could be here too, *mon frere.* Now you must write to them and tell them they are grandparents again. They will be happy that there is now a *petite fille* to compete with the boys in the family."

Henri smiled. "I will write a letter and send it when I go to town next."

The baby began to cry softly, so Catey took Amy's arm and helped her back to the small, one room cabin. The brothers lingered by the stream. Henri sat on a jagged rock and swiped his hand in the cool, clear water.

"How our lives have changed, Francois. I cannot believe I am now a father. It scares me. What am I to do? I don't know how to be a father."

Francois leaned over and touched his brother's arm. "You will be fine, *frere*. Trust me, you will learn as you go. Besides, you have Amy, and you have Catey and me to help. You have always loved children. All will be fine. You will see. What is that you always say? *Ne pas craindre quel est pour venir. L'embrasser*."

Henri gazed into the water. "Do not fear what is to come. Embrace it. Yes, brother. I know you are right."

Francois searched for the right words. "One day, we will take our children and go back to see Mama and Papa. How proud they will be. I say if the great river brought us here, so the great river can take us back." He thought a change in the conversation might do his brother some good. "Do you remember how we struggled to learn the English language when we first came to America?"

Henri nodded. "I struggle still at times. Amy often must tell me how to say a word or a sentence. That first village we visited...do you remember? We were almost killed because I said the wrong thing. They thought we were like the rest – liars and thieves. Your smile, it convinced them."

"I do have a nice smile, *oui*?" Francois cocked his head and shot Henri a grin. "But they were good people. They just needed to know us. And our pelts, they traded for them very fast. Papa taught us well."

The sun felt warm on their backs, and Henri watched as the swirling waters tugged a maple leaf over his outstretched hand. He turned and looked at the cabin. "I hope she will be well. I do not think I could care for this child by myself."

"Do not say such things," Francois said. "She will be fine. Catey will see to that. Besides, Amy is a strong woman. You know, I still laugh when I think back to when we were in their village and you wanted to help the other women plant the garden.

You said you were tired of just sitting watching and waiting for my arm to heal. The women told you it was not for guests of their village to work, but you asked the elders for permission anyway." He chuckled. "You think you are so smart, but I know why you wanted to garden."

"So I could be close to her," Henri said, pulling his hand from the water and wiping it on his pants. He realized his brother was teasing him. "Oh, so you accuse me of trickery? You, *mon frere*, you pretended to be sick so Catey would stay close."

"How can you say such things?" Henri rolled his eyes. "I *was* sick. But she is so beautiful I almost wished to stay that way."

"We are lucky men," Henri said.

"Henri!" Catey called from the cabin. "Amy is asking for you."

Francois slapped his brother on the back. "Very lucky, indeed."

Chapter 2

August 3, 1858
Oregon County, Missouri

"But I want to go with him. He said I could go. He wants to show me how to track animals and he wants me to help him with his traps." The little girl stood firm on the hard, dusty ground and looked up at her mother.

Amy picked up the hoe. "He said you could go with him some day, not today. Victoria, you are too young. And I need you here with me. We must weed the garden today, and the horses need tending."

"I am not too young. And Aunt Catey said she was coming over to help you. Mama, our clan is the Deer Clan. You say we're the keepers of the deer in the forest and that our people run very fast and track the deer. I can run fast. I want to learn to track, too. It is my duty. Daniel and Jesse have already been in the forest. They tease me because I don't know how to track animals yet. It's my turn now."

Francois' twin boys, Daniel and Jesse, were a year older than Victoria. They went hunting and trapping with Francois and Henri often, and found plenty of opportunities to remind their cousin of her lack of experience. Victoria was determined to change that.

Henri sat on the edge of the porch and pulled on his beaver skin boots. He grinned at his wife. *What a smart daughter I have. She makes a good point.* With his most stern father face he said, "Victoria, do not argue with your mother. Now, I forgot my water skin. I think it is on the table. Fetch it and fill it for me *sil vous plait*."

Victoria raced up the steps and into the cabin. When she was out of ear shot, Henri turned to Amy. "She is right, you know. Deer Clan members plant crops and care for the animals. Is this correct?"

"Yes, you know that," Amy replied.

"Well, she knows how to plant the crops and feed and brush the animals. Now she must learn what *I* do." He grabbed her by her waist and pulled her close. "I promise to take good care of her, *ma chere*. I want to teach her to track and hunt and one day make fine furs, like my papa taught me. We will not go far."

Amy's eyes widened. "She's my only child, Henri, and she's not yet six years old. I want no harm to come to her."

"She is my only child, too," he said, stroking her long hair. "But she needs to learn the ways of the forest, of her clan. How can she ever travel from this mountain if she does not grow?"

She knew he was right. He held her close and kissed her forehead. She lingered, feeling the warmth of his strong arms.

"It is her time," he whispered.

She turned and saw Victoria running toward them and reluctantly sighed. "You go today. But you must mind your papa."

Victoria rushed to her and hugged her tightly. "Thank you Mama! I promise. I'll run very fast and bring home something good for supper."

Amy smiled up at Henri. "She has a strong will."

"Like her mama," he said with a wink.

Amy touched her finger to his cheek. He bent to kiss her. His mustache felt soft and full on her lips. She stepped back from him. "Before you go, let me put some Goldenseal on her. It should keep the mosquitoes off."

She looked at both of them and wagged her finger. "And I want you two back before dark. You, child, have a reading lesson."

Henri and Victoria walked into the dense woods. Victoria's eyes were wide and her head spun in all directions, trying to absorb everything.

"Why is it so dark, Papa?"

He held her hand tightly. *"Ne pas craindre quel est pour venir. L'embrasser."*

"I'm not afraid, Papa." She continued to scan the unfamiliar area. "I'll be alright."

"You see, it is only because there are so many tall trees that the sun cannot shine through. It is very cool on your skin, is it not?"

"Yes. It feels good. Do the animals like it here?"

"Oh, they do very much. When you learn the ways of the forest, you will also love being here. It is quiet and very peaceful. But you must be aware, *ma petite*. There are also many dangers here. You must not go too far ahead of me. It will worry your mama. And we don't want that, now, do we?"

Despite the warning, Victoria strained to pull her hand from his so she could explore more. "When do we find the animals?" she asked.

He stopped and knelt down in front of her. "Look at me, Victoria. This is your first lesson. When you track and hunt the animals, you must be very, very quiet and walk very, very slow. Do not make noise and do not run. Do you understand?"

Victoria stopped. "Yes Papa. Do we sneak up on them?"

He smiled inwardly. "Something like that. Let me show you."

Victoria bobbed excitedly and giggled, her long, black ponytail danced on her back.

They walked to a nearby maple sapling; a thin branch hung loosely from the trunk.

"See how this branch is broke here?" He asked.

"Did an animal do that?"

"Perhaps. Why don't we ask the tree? Did you know trees can talk?"

"Oh, Papa, no they can't."

He cupped his hand to his ear. "If you look closely and listen very hard, you will hear them speak. Shhh. Did you hear that?"

Victoria leaned close to the tree, listening for a faint whisper. "What is it saying?"

"The tree is telling us that something has walked past and it came too close. The branch broke when they hit it. Do you see?"

"Yes."

He pointed to a tuft of animal hair stuck in the bark of the tree. "Now, look here. Do you see this hair?"

Victoria nodded. "Yes."

"Remember to always look for this. It will tell you about the animal."

He pulled the tuft from the tree and held it out. "Now, three things tell me it was a deer. Do you know how I know this?"

She shook her head.

"First, the tree told me so."

"Oh, Papa!"

He grinned. "It is true. And I also know because the hair is way up high on the tree. It could not be a rabbit or a fox. They are not that tall, are they?"

"You know they aren't, Papa," she laughed. "They're this tall," she said and held her hand down to the ground indicating her version of a rabbit's height, which to Henri looked more like the height of a chipmunk, and he stifled a smile.

"Very good." He held the animal hair close to her face. "The other things that say it is a deer are the color and the feel of the hair. See how it is brown. Now feel how stiff it is." She stroked the tuft and nodded. "We will keep this hair so you can tell the difference between a deer and a raccoon or a rabbit." He handed her the hair, and she placed it carefully in a small leather pouch at her waist.

"Now, look down on the ground. Do you see these marks in the dirt?" he said referring to the hoof prints made by a passing deer.

"What are those?" she asked.

"These are the footprints of a deer. And I think a big deer, too because the prints are sunk deep into the ground."

She stared wide-eyed at the marks.

They knelt down to get a closer look. "Remember these markings, Eagle Eyes. They will tell you that a deer has been here."

"I will, Papa," she replied slowly, still absorbing the detail of the hoof prints.

Satisfied that she would remember her first lesson, he proceeded. "Now, Eagle Eyes, just because you do not see the animal here does not mean it has gone far away. You must always look for the animal. And smell for the animal." He raised his head and made a pronounced sniffing sound.

"Remember that wild animals are just that – they are wild," Henri said.

"The deer aren't mean. They always run away when I try to talk to them."

"But they can kill you if they sense danger, like if you come close to their babies. Any animal can be dangerous and mean, even the birds. Remember that we are in their house when we walk in the woods. We must respect the wild animals. That way we will stay safe."

Henri showed Victoria how to find and follow other animal tracks in the dense underbrush, and they spent the morning identifying animals by what they left behind. They found different footprints in the soft, damp earth; deep prints spoke of a heavy animal, a wolf, deer or cougar, while faint tracks meant a lighter animal, maybe a rabbit or a squirrel or a raccoon had passed by. But she was also fascinated by the various types of animal droppings they encountered. "I thought all animal poop was the same," she said giggling.

"Now you know the difference," he said and watched as she made her way down a narrow path, her eyes scanning every direction for clues.

He marveled at how quickly she was learning and wondered how she could have grown up so fast. He stood locked briefly in the past as memories of her birth came flooding back...

He had been concerned that Amy's labor was lasting too long. Catey reassured him that some babies took longer than others to make their grand entrance and that Amy was doing her best. Finally the child had arrived, and Amy lay on the cot, exhausted. He sat down next to her and kissed her and they gently embraced. Catey had wrapped the child in a warm blanket; the infant rested next to her mother.

The medicine woman said to him, "Henri, she needs her rest." She knelt down beside Amy and gently brushed her hair from her sweating brow. "You and Henri have made a beautiful daughter, but for now I want you to lie still. Henri will take her."

Henri stood and shook his head. "*Non*, I do not know how to hold a child. I might drop her."

"Then it's time you learned. Now, put out your arms," Catey said. She showed him how to cradle his new daughter. His large hands and chest engulfed the tiny package, and he grinned proudly, albeit nervously.

He then nodded toward his wife. "Will she be alright?"

Catey shrugged. "She had a hard labor and delivery. I'm concerned that she's still bleeding heavily. I'm going to give her some buckeye bark and chestnut to drink. I pray that it will work, but I fear this child you hold will likely be the only one you'll have." She glanced back at Amy, who was already asleep.

Francois burst through the cabin door. "Let me see this child." He pulled the blanket back from her tiny face. "Look at all that black hair. I hope it is a girl. Is it?"

"Oui," Henri replied.

"She looks like her mother. Thank heaven for that."

"Francois Levalier!" Catey said in a loud whisper. "Can't you see Amy is sleeping? Be quiet, or I'll pack your bags and put them on the porch!"

Francois turned to his wife with an impish grin, then looked back at his brother and lowered his voice. "She…she is so tiny. My boys were not that tiny, were they? I forgot how small they are. Henri, did you ever think this was to be?"

"*Non*," Henri replied staring in disbelief at his daughter. "It was good that you got hurt."

"Good? You mock my suffering?" he scoffed in feigned disbelief.

"We would never have met our women if you hadn't been hurt."

"This is true, brother." He looked back at Catey. "My Catey. She is a good wife, and medicine woman. I owe her my life."

The child grunted and squirmed in Henri's arms.

"Look – she is already strong. A born hunter and trapper!" Francois said.

Catey tickled the tiny feet protruding from the soft cotton blanket. "And she'll be a good farmer and *nv-wa-ti a-ge-yv*."

Both men stared at Catey with wrinkled brows.

She shook her head. "Don't you remember any words in our language? She'll be a good medicine woman, too..."

Suddenly Victoria's excited voice shook him from his memories and brought him back to the forest. "Papa, come see! I think I found another trail!"

He found her pointing to animal tracks in the soft dirt, and laughed in amazement. "You are certainly true to your name, Eagle Eyes. We named you that for the color of your eyes, but our Creator is wise. Those eagle eyes, they see everything!"

Apparently she didn't hear him because she was already moving down the trail on another quest.

He called after her, "Eagle Eyes...Victoria, not so far. Come back now."

"Look, we found this rabbit in one of Papa's traps!" She held up her prize. "He's going to help me skin it. Can we eat it for supper?"

"I hope you thanked the animal for giving up its life for you. For allowing you to eat its meat and use its fur," Amy said.

Victoria's smile faded to a more serious face. "Yes, Mama, I did."

Amy knelt down and caressed her daughter's face. "Then I have a stew just waiting for that very special rabbit."

She looked up at Henri. "You two look very pleased with yourselves. It seems she learned much today, husband."

"It is like she has been in the forest all her life," he said as Victoria danced around the cabin.

Victoria could hardly contain her excitement. "And Papa says we can go out again tomorrow. If you say yes, I mean. But he told me about the traps. Even if we're going hunting, we have to be sure and check the traps every day. We don't want the animal to suffer. And he said traps are very strong and they can hurt me if I'm not careful. Papa let me touch one of them. The teeth were very sharp. He says Uncle Francois was hurt by one."

Amy replied. "Yes, he caught his arm in one of his traps one time. It was a deep cut and he was bleeding very badly. He and your papa came to our village. Aunt Catey used her medicine on his cut and it got better."

"Is that when they got married?"

"Well, it was a little later than that," Amy said.

"Tell me about how you met Papa," Victoria said.

"Maybe later, after you finish your reading lesson. We don't have time for that now. Papa will skin the rabbit. You must brush and feed the horses and then help me with supper."

"But, Mama."

"Do as I say, Victoria. You can learn to skin the next rabbit. Hurry now."

The child pouted briefly, but ran out of the cabin to the nearby enclosure where two horses stood in wait. Their ears perked up when they caught her scent.

"Chief…Bear," she said to the horses. "I went to the forest today with Papa and I learned to track wild animals. It was fun. Papa said I was a good tracker."

The horses nickered softly, expecting a treat. She ran to the garden and pulled two carrots. Both animals quickly sucked them up, and then nodded, asking for more.

"That's enough for now. You'll spoil your supper."

She found the grooming brush and began to work on Chief first, as he was the biggest and took more time. "We found a rabbit in one of the traps and are going to eat it for supper. Then Papa is going to show me how to make a beautiful pelt, one that he'll sell. He says he'll give me the money. I like hunting and trapping. Papa says I'm learning very fast."

When she finished with Chief, she turned her attention to Bear and continued her lecture on the nuances of tracking and trapping. After completing her task, she put away the brush, poured a pile of corn on the ground, and filled the water trough with fresh water from the stream.

"Maybe we can go for a ride tomorrow," she said and skipped back toward the cabin.

She stopped in the garden and picked several ripe tomatoes; they would make a nice addition to the supper table. She called out to the nearby cabin. "Aunt Catey, I'm taking tomatoes. I'll bring you some, too."

Catey stepped out onto her front porch, and Victoria ran to meet her. "Thank you, Victoria. They'll taste good with my *ga-na-tsi*," Catey said, referring to a delicious soup made with beans, corn and hickory nuts. "Are you coming over tomorrow? I want to show you another way to use the blue powder and how to make Sassafras tea."

"I can after I do my chores. Is that alright?"

"Of course."

"But, I can't stay long. Me and Papa are going tracking again."

Catey cocked her head. "You'd better not let your mother hear you talk that way. You must speak proper English, Victoria."

Victoria thought for a moment. "I mean, Papa and I are going tracking again."

Catey smiled. "That is exciting. You're going to be a great hunter and trapper, my little Eagle Eyes."

"I know. Papa says so, too. Today we found a rabbit in one of his traps. We're going to eat it for supper. And Papa showed me how to find animal tracks and how to follow them. Did you know that animals have different poop?"

Catey laughed. "I did know that. You're learning a great deal."

Victoria nodded. "Mama says I should learn everything I can. That way I'll be a strong Cherokee *a-ge-yv*."

"And your mama is right. All Cherokee women are strong. How is your reading coming along?"

"Papa bought some books when he went to town and I can already read all of them."

"Well done! But if you're having rabbit for supper, I think you should be getting home. I think I smell it all the way over here."

A gentle breeze wafted across the front porch; the night air was cool and refreshing. Victoria sat between her parents and watched Chief and Bear bed down for the night.

"Mama, can we sing?" Victoria asked.

"What would you like to sing?" Amy put her arm around her daughter.

"About the warriors. Papa, you sing, too."

Henri didn't share their zeal for singing; he had a difficult time with the melody and tempo of the Cherokee songs. "Maybe I will just listen, *ma fille*. I don't sing so good and I want to hear your sweet voices."

They sat in the waning light and sang of brave Cherokee warriors who vowed not to kill women, old men and children when they battled their enemies. Next they sang about the ancients who scared a huge dog that was eating all their corn meal. The dog jumped into the sky, and the meal spilled from its mouth and became the Milky Way. Amy smiled contentedly when Victoria sang of Yowa, the Great Creator, and how he gave fire and smoke to the Cherokee.

When Victoria finished her song, she looked at Amy. "Can we go back to your village one day?"

"I'd like that," Amy said. "But right now, it's time for you to go to bed."

"But you promised to tell me about you and Papa."

"We'll do that tomorrow night."

"Please," she pleaded. "Just a little."

Henri reached over and pulled Victoria onto his lap. "*Juste en peu.* Then off to bed you go. Now, let me see…I met your mama when me and Francois came to her village."

Victoria sat up and looked directly at him. "You must speak proper English. It's Francois and *I*, Papa."

Henri patted her on the top of her head. "Yes, you are correct. Francois and I came to your mama's village. Your uncle and I, we traveled from Canada, from our home in Toronto. Canada is a country far to the north of here. My mama, your *grandmere*, she is a kind, beautiful woman. Everyone loves her. Your *grandpere*, he taught Francois and me how to hunt and trap and make wonderful pelts for everyone to buy. For a while there were plenty of animals. But then there were so many trappers in Canada. Most animals are gone now. So, we left and came to America. We rode on rafts down the great Mississippi River and went south to follow the animal trails. We trapped many and made the pelts to sell and trade. That is how we make our living. But most animals are gone from here now, too. When they are all gone, I am afraid Francois and I will have to find other things to do with our time."

He frowned briefly before continuing, knowing that what he said would probably come to pass. "Now, one day, when your uncle was trying to set a trap, like a silly fool he put his hand down in between the trap's teeth. Something happened and it snapped shut on his arm. The teeth sunk into his skin, almost to the bone. He was hurt bad and needed a doctor. We were lucky to be close to your mama's village."

Amy said, "Catey put Yarrow powder on his arm and wrapped it. Then she came to my house and told me about two handsome strangers with a funny-sounding last name. She asked me if I wanted to meet them."

"So you went to see them?" Victoria yawned.

"Of course. What woman wouldn't want to meet two handsome men?" Her eyes met Henri's. "When I met him, I told him he had beautiful blue eyes."

"She melted my heart," Henri said looking at his wife. "I was taken by her beauty and she was very…how do you say it? Very bold. She stood tall and held her head high."

"Your papa and Uncle Francois stayed in our village for many weeks so his arm could heal. I liked your papa and was very glad he stayed," Amy said.

Suddenly Henri sat up and looked at Amy. "Wait. You think my last name is funny? Levalier? What is so funny about Levalier?"

Amy laughed softly and kissed his cheek. "It was strange to me then, and I couldn't wrap my tongue around it. But it didn't stop me from wanting to be with you."

Henri met his wife's gaze for a tender moment, then looked back at his daughter. "Anyway, your mama chose me to be her husband, and Catey chose Francois. The four of us got married on the same day, and the people in the village had a big celebration for us."

"What do you do when you get married?" Victoria asked.

Henri glanced over at Amy. "Well…we stood in front of the sacred fire and the priest covered each of us with a blue blanket."

Amy added, "Then the priest gave us his blessing. And when that was done, he took the two blue blankets away and covered us with one big white blanket. That meant that your papa and I had left our separate lives and joined together as one."

"Then did you leave and come here?"

"*Non*, we waited until the snows melted in the spring. Then we crossed the great river and came here. Your uncle and I, we bought this land and built our houses," Henri said. "And so here we are."

Victoria snuggled into his soft, deerskin shirt and closed her eyes. "Is Canada like here?"

"Sort of. There are lots of tall trees, but it is much colder in the winter," he replied.

"I don't like being cold. Do you?" she mumbled.

"*Non*, it is much warmer here in the winter than it is back in Canada. But the summers, I think they are hotter here. Maybe one day we will go back and see Canada and your grandparents. Would you like that?"

When she didn't respond, he looked down at his little hunter. She was fast asleep.

"I think the forest and her papa wore her out," Amy whispered.

Chapter 3

Present day
Affton, Missouri

The phone was ringing as Julie walked in the back door.

"I'll get it," she called. "Hello?"

She looked into the living room. Mike was focused on the TV. *Don't know why I even say anything. He's deaf on game day.*

"Julie? It's Maggie from Dr. Norton's office. I'm calling with the results from the blood test and bone scan you had Wednesday."

"Hi Maggie. Well, how bad is it?"

"Actually, it's not all bad. Your total cholesterol is 220, which is a little higher than doctor wants, but your HDL and triglycerides are within normal range. That's good. However, your bone density scan shows that you're beginning to lose some of your bone mass in your pelvis area."

"That's *not* good," Julie replied.

"No, and I know you don't want to hear this, but our charts show you've put on about 25 pounds over the last few years."

"You're not telling me anything my jeans haven't told me already," she laughed. It was true, and Julie had been ignoring it. She took a deep breath. "So, now what?"

"Well, we need to get you started on a statin to lower your cholesterol. It would also be a good idea to begin an aerobic exercise program for your weight control. Do you exercise now?"

"When I can," Julie said. "But I'm not into leotards and sweatbands and struttin' my stuff. I'm not gonna go to some meat market."

Maggie replied. "I hear ya. If you don't want to go that route, skip the leotards and try walking. It's a wonderful way to burn calories. And you might want to try lifting some weights. It strengthens your bones. That's what I do."

"You lift weights?" Julie asked.

"Uh huh. You don't have to turn into a pile of muscles. The key is to use lighter weights. Check out one of the gyms or fit clubs. They all have women's programs. And you can get calcium supplements with Vitamin D at the drugstore."

"I guess I can thank good old menopause for this," Julie sighed.

"Amen to that," Maggie said. "I think you'll notice a big difference if you keep up a regular exercise program. It not only keeps us strong, but minimizes those hot flashes – I call 'em my private summers. And research says it helps with the gray matter, too. Now, which pharmacy should we call for your statin prescription?"

Julie quickly ran through her options. "Can I make a deal with Dr. Norton? I'd like to try to get my weight and cholesterol under control without the drugs. I really hate taking pills. I feel like once you get started on one, you find yourself on the pill merry-go-round. Can you see if he'll give me six months on a diet and exercise program. Then can I come back in and see if it's working?

"Let me check with the doctor." She put Julie on hold for a few minutes. "He says that would be fine with him if you promise to come back in six months."

"I promise. Thanks, Maggie." She hung up the phone and walked into the den. "Well, that's just perfect," she sighed heavily and plopped down beside Mike, jarring him from the game.

"What?" he asked.

"I knew it!"

"What did you knew?"

"That was the doctor's office with results from my physical. My cholesterol's too high, my bone density's getting low and I need to lose twenty five pounds! Menopause sucks! I'm only fifty two, but I refuse to end up like my mom."

"Your mom didn't die from being overweight." Mike said with a dead pan expression.

"I know that, silly. It was the osteoporosis. They want me to walk more. Get more exercise. Jeez, you'd think marching around that classroom all day chasing after students would be enough, but apparently not. What I need to do is get my big butt in gear and lose some of this fat."

"C'mon, babe, you're not fat. And I like your butt." Mike reached around her crossed leg to pat her rear-end.

"Well I don't," she said, smacking his hand. "And I plan on being a pain in yours for a long time."

"Oh no, not another thirty years of this." He gasped and gripped his chest.

"You can't fool me, Michael Alexander. I know where I stand. Somewhere between your Harley, your poker, your cars and your kids."

"Yeah, somewhere in there," he said staring at the television.

She reached up and mussed his hair, and he grabbed her arms and pulled her to him. They snuggled down into the cushions.

"You're missing your game," she said.

"More important stuff right now." He kissed her neck and ran his fingers through her soft, curly blond hair.

"Do we have time before the kids get here?" she whispered.

"Always time for you babe."

"We can't stay long, Mom," Ashley said. "It's Brandon's brother's birthday, and they're having a party for him."

Julie liked Brandon. He and Ashley had been together for over a year now, and they seemed to match up well, Ashley with her degree in graphic design and Brandon a computer geek. He doted on Ashley, and Julie figured it never hurt to know someone who could patch up the old desktop in the back room. It wouldn't surprise her if an engagement announcement was in the near future.

"Me either," Chris said. "I told Valerie we'd go out for dinner at that new Cajun restaurant. You guys wanna come?"

Mike glanced at Julie who shook her head. "Ah, we'll take a rain check," he said. "So how's work?"

"It's good," Chris replied.

Mike smiled. Chris was a motor head, just like his dad. "No thought of coming to work for me?"

"I don't know, Dad. I like it at Royal Imports. I'm learning a lot, and nobody treats me special. I'd be afraid if I came to work for you I'd be 'the boss' son.' And I don't want that. Not just yet."

"Well, you *would* be the boss' son. That's okay. I liked working there too when I was your age. Maybe when you decide you've learned enough, you can head up my shop. Then I can retire and leave you with the headaches."

"I'll keep that in mind," Chris said, grinning.

"So, what are you two doing this summer now that school's out?" Brandon asked.

"Well," Julie said. "Mike's wearing a hole in the leather recliner when he's not at work, and I'm thinking of starting an exercise program." She didn't want to bore them with the sordid details.

"Hey, Mom, did you ever finish the family tree?" Ashley asked.

"No, not yet," Julie replied.

"How come?"

"I'm stuck and need somebody to help."

"What are you stuck on?"

"Not what…who. Your great-great-grandmother, Victoria."

Mike turned to Ashley. "Now why'd you go reminding her about that? I don't know why she sees the need to dig up ancestors. She wasted her entire summer break last year on that family tree junk."

"So? What difference does it make to you?" Julie glared at him. "Besides, I didn't waste anything, and it's not junk. Just because you don't care about your ancestors doesn't mean I can't care about mine. I want to know more about who I am, and where I came from."

He looked at Julie and shrugged his shoulders. "So every time you get a few days off, you're running all over creation trying to find your dead relatives."

"Sometimes things are easy to find, and sometimes they aren't. You'd know that if you tried to do your family tree."

"And what's it gonna get you? A piece of paper that says who fathered who. Well, la de fricken da."

Julie didn't like arguing in front of the kids, so she turned and walked into the kitchen. "Anybody need something to drink? I made lemonade and it's calling my name."

With the kids gone and Mike napping after his early afternoon delight, Julie wandered down the hall toward the computer room. It was too hot to walk outside, and Ashley had re-ignited the family tree flame. *I'll try some other genealogy sights. Maybe I'll get lucky.*

While the old computer hummed to life, Julie opened the bottom drawer of the file cabinet and pulled out a large folder labeled "Mom."

"Well, Victoria, let's see what I find on you today," she said.

She had previously worked on several genealogy websites, and using the name Victoria Yochem, her great-grandmother's married name, found a little information, including Victoria's birth and death dates, as well as the names of her parents, Henri and Amy Levalier.

Today Julie thought she would try to find out more about the man named Henri Levalier. First up, she typed Henri's full name into the search engine. The computer stuttered momentarily and then flashed several results for the name Levalier. She clicked on the first one in the bunch, and read a brief bio on Pierre Levalier, a renowned seventeenth century artisan from France. *Nope, not him.* The next three websites provided information on Levalier coffee and coffee makers. *Nope, not here either.*

She was getting more frustrated every time she tried to delve deeper into her bloodline. She exhausted the sites for Levalier, and opted to try another angle. She went to FamilySearch.org and searched for her maternal grandfather, Robert Yochem. She found a birth and death date for Robert and a marriage to Anna Simmons, her grandmother. Robert's father, her great-grandfather, was named Rogers Yochem. She also found a marriage notice between Rogers Yochem and Victoria Levalier. She copied and pasted the information into her family pedigree document, the one she planned to use to create a book about her family's history and give it as a Christmas gift to the kids.

"Now I might be getting somewhere," she said. Her thoughts were interrupted by the phone. She was so focused on her research that she jumped six inches off the chair when it rang. She chuckled to herself and took a deep, cleansing breath.

"Hello."

"What's up sis?" It was Matt.

"Hello brother dear. What's up with you?"

"You sound bummed."

"I am. First off, the phone just scared the you-know-what out of me. I almost jumped out of my chair."

"Glad to know I haven't lost my touch."

"Secondly, the doctor says I need to lose twenty five pounds, but it's too hot to go outside."

"Twenty five pounds? That's all? You should be able to do that easy."

"Very funny. I wish. You got Dad's genes. You'll never get fat."

"Hey, a little exercise and a few salads and you'll be skinny in no time."

"I'm glad you think so."

She loved to hang out with her younger brother, but it hadn't always been that way. As a kid he was forever sticking his nose in her business. He was like a little detective; constantly asking questions, like why was she doing this, or how come she did that.

She answered his questions with, "Why do you want to know? You writin' a book?" It didn't stop him, though. He seemed to relish driving her to the brink of insanity.

They ran around with different crowds in high school and pretty much went their separate ways after graduation. They exchanged the usual birthday and Christmas cards, only seeing each other on special occasions. It wasn't that they didn't love each other, but time and busy schedules simply distanced their relationship. Matt's career in law enforcement was taking off; his obsession with asking questions had finally landed him the perfect job, that of detective with the Alton Missouri Police Department. His wife, Rachel, worked for the Alton Medical Clinic as a nutritionist.

Then their parents died. Two funerals in two years were eye-openers. They reevaluated their priorities, and both decided family was important and it was time to be a family again. They started making time for each other, even if it was just a weekend visit. Julie was glad to have her brother back, and she and Rachel became instant friends.

"To what do I owe the pleasure?" Julie asked.

"Well, we had an idea. Why don't you two drive down to Big Forest and go camping with us? Rachel wants to go hiking. You could go with her. Might help you lose some of that weight you're griping about."

"You guys are just exercise freaks."

"Guess I get that from Dad, too. We've got a few days of vacation time coming, and it would be fun. It's always cooler by the river, ya know."

"What, no bad guys to chase?"

"Too hot for 'em, I guess."

She mulled over her options...*Hmm, stay home and fret about the fat, or do something about it*. It was clear which option she needed to take. "Sure, why not. I'll tell Mike. I bet he can get Friday off and drive down for a three day weekend. I'll pack the bus and call the campground and make reservations."

"Already made 'em," Matt said.

"So you're psychic now? From when to when?"

"No, I just thought you might need a break from the heat. Anyway, Monday to Sunday. That okay with you?"

"Works for me. I'll leave Monday morning and see you there."

"Okay. Remember, lots of lettuce and your hiking stuff."

"Yeah, yeah, lots of lettuce," she replied rolling her eyes. She hung up, turned off the computer and walked back down the hall to the den.

"Victoria, you're going to have to wait a little longer," she said.

"Who was that?" Mike asked sleepily.

"Matt. He wants us to go camping at Big Forest Campground next week. Rachel and I can go hiking, too. I told him we'd go. I'll go Monday and set up. Think you can get Friday off for a three day weekend?"

"Sure, I've got meetings all this week, but I think I can swing it. Nap time's over anyway. I'll help you get the bus ready."

"Gee, thanks hon," she quipped. "It's nice to know I can always count on you."

"Anything for you, sweet cheeks."

Chapter 4

Summer, 1862
Oregon County, Missouri

"Victoria, please come and help me with these baskets," Amy called.

The morning air was warm and hung heavy in the trees. It had been that way for the last week or so. She hoped it would cool off soon, maybe even rain. She seemed to be sweating more and for some unknown reason was feeling weak.

"Do you want me to weave them with you?" Victoria asked.

"Why don't you make the stains for me? I'm working with white oak today."

"What should I use?"

"We'll try the walnut bark and some bloodroot today. They'll make pretty brown and orange colors to go with the white of the oak. I thought you were going with your papa today to help him with his traps." Amy said.

"I told him that I was going to stay here with you. But when he comes back, I promised I would help him skin the pelts."

Amy smiled softly, trying to mask her relief that Victoria was staying behind. She could use her daughter's help, but she knew Victoria's heart would be in the forest today, as it always was. She said, "You make such beautiful pelts. Papa says he gets more money for yours than he does for his."

"Yes, but I think he just says that. I'm not that good, not yet. I will be soon, though. And he says I can go with him one day to town. Then I can buy something with my money."

"Your papa will be going down to where the river narrows today, and it will be late when he returns. You may not be able to skin pelts today."

"But I can finish my chores after we dye the baskets. Then I'll help you with the garden and with supper. If we eat as soon as he returns, maybe we can work on the pelts before it gets dark."

"That sounds like a busy day for you. Are you sure you don't want to go with your papa? It'll probably be less work for you, my dear."

"That's okay, Mama. Besides, you need my help."

"And I'll gladly take it. I'm a little tired today."

Victoria worried about her mother. Simple chores seemed to wear her out these days, and Victoria wondered if her mother might be pregnant. Sometimes Victoria heard soft moans coming from her parents' bed. She knew what was happening. She had seen wild animals do it in the forest. Papa said the animals were making babies. Whenever she heard her parents, she always stifled her giggles and prayed that her parents would make a baby sister or brother for her. She hoped it was actually happening this time.

The water sloshed into the trough as Victoria poured it from the bucket. Chief and Bear drank deeply, sucking noisily through their teeth. She watched their ears bob with each gulp. "You two are thirsty. It's going to be another hot day. I'll go get you more," Victoria said and picked up the bucket. "But I can't stay and talk because I have to help Mama with the garden."

After she watered the horses, she bounced up onto the porch where Amy sat waiting.

"Ready for the garden, Mama?"

Amy nodded and started to stand but suddenly sank back into her chair. Victoria rushed to her.

"Mama? Are you alright?"

Amy said, "I'm just feeling a little tired, dear. I think I need to go lie down for a bit. We'll work in the garden later, after I rest."

Victoria felt her mother shivering and knew it wasn't a baby; something was terribly wrong. She had to almost carry Amy the last few steps to the bed. Pulling the covers up, Victoria felt her mother's forehead and face; it was hot and damp.

"Mama?" Victoria shook her mother's shoulder, but Amy wasn't responding.

Her eyes filled with tears, and she turned and ran in search of her aunt Catey.

The medicine woman used all of the remedies she knew, from Sassafras and willow bark tea to concoctions of flax, horsemint, feverwort and snake root, but nothing seemed to help. She treated Amy's fever for three days, never leaving her side, chanting and praying to the spirits for her return to good health.

On the fourth day, Amy's breathing became labored and a rattling sound came from her chest. Catey knew her sister-in-law was dying. She motioned for Henri and Victoria to follow her outside to the porch.

"I can do no more for her. None of my medicines are helping, and the spirits are not willing to listen to my pleas."

"But you're a great medicine woman," Victoria cried. "You have to make her better."

Catey shook her head. "Sometimes my medicines aren't strong enough. I'm sorry, Eagle Eyes. You must be strong now. She won't live much longer. Go, be near her now, and say your peace."

Victoria went inside and sat on the edge of her mother's bed. Tears streamed down her face.

"Don't blame Catey. She has tried her best," Amy whispered. "I have so much to tell you, Eagle Eyes, but we have no more time. I'm going to the Spirit World soon."

Victoria had been told about the Spirit World. She knew that was where her people went when they died. She pressed her face to her mother's chest and sobbed. "Don't go, Mama. Papa needs you. I need you."

"Hush now. Please don't cry." Amy stroked Victoria's hair and whispered in her ear. "My beautiful child, listen to me. You must be strong, for yourself and for your papa. I promise I'll watch over you. Speak my name and...my spirit will always be close. We'll see each other soon. I love you so much, Eagle Eyes."

"And I love you, too, Mama."

Amy looked up at Catey through eyes brimming with tears. "Promise me you'll show her what I cannot. Teach her all that she needs to know. Teach her our ways."

"I promise, Little Squirrel. I'll teach her," Catey said tearfully.

Henri knelt down next to Amy and held her tightly; she didn't notice his silent tears.

"Take care of our daughter," Amy whispered to him. "I'll wait for you in the Spirit World, my love."

He held her hands tightly, never wanting to let go, and looked deep into her eyes. "Stay with us," he pleaded.

"I can't. It's my time to go."

He lifted her into his arms and held her. Her breathing was shallow. She slipped into unconsciousness and he felt her go limp in his embrace. He gently laid her down and held her hands.

Catey leaned over his shoulder and looked at Amy. "She is near her time, Henri. It won't be much longer."

"I will stay with her," he replied.

Henri felt Catey's hand on his shoulder. With a small start, he realized he had fallen asleep. It was morning and he was still sitting beside Amy, holding her hands in his. A soft, cool rain arrived during the night and droplets fell slowly from the overhanging trees. It was as if the sky was weeping.

Catey knelt down and felt Amy's face. "Henri, she is gone." She hugged him gently. Victoria joined their embrace and the three of them wept together.

Catey finally stood and wiped her eyes. "We must act quickly. Henri, I need you to go tell Francois and Daniel and Jesse to come."

She turned to Victoria. "Eagle Eyes, we have so much to do to send your mama to the Spirit World. Go into the forest and find a willow tree. I want you to dig up some of the root and bring it back here and boil it in water. Make a big pot. It's very important for the ceremony. Go now. Hurry!"

On any other day Victoria would have loved to be in the dark forest, would have found comfort in the escape - but not today. She trudged in blindly, wiping away tears. The rain had stopped, and the forest again began to bustle with life. Squirrels jumped from tree to tree, birds squawked at her presence, rabbits scurried in front of her, but she didn't stop to watch. She was consumed with grief. Her mother was gone.

Blindly she slogged deeper into the bushes. The dampness smothered her; she was oblivious to the thorns tearing at her shirt and scratching her legs.

She felt as if she was in a bad dream. "Mama, please. Come back!" She tripped on a large tree root and fell to the cool, damp earth, landing on her knees. She sobbed uncontrollably; her tears flooded the ground. Suddenly she felt a wave of calm settle over her, like a comforting hand on her shoulder, and it seemed to give her strength. She stood up, wiped her eyes and looked around. She heard the nearby stream and went to it to wash away her tears and some of the mud on her hands and arms.

When she finished, she said to herself, "Stop crying Victoria! Mama wouldn't want it. Cherokee women are strong and brave. You have a job to do. Now, find the tree!"

Eventually she found a small willow suitable to her task. Her fingers dug into the soft, sandy soil and pulled up a section of root. She snapped it off and clutched it gently as she made her way back. Approaching the cabin, she saw her father and her uncle Francois digging the grave. She ran to them and fell into Henri's arms; fresh tears ran down her cheeks as the reality of her mother's death sunk deeper.

Henri pulled from the embrace and said, "We will bury her here in the shade by the porch. That way she can watch over our work. We must be sure we do it right." His thin smile masked his grief.

Victoria turned away from her father's sadness and said, "Papa, I need to take this root to Aunt Catey and help her." She left the men to their task and rushed into the cabin.

Both families stood in the tiny cabin next to Amy's lifeless body. Catey looked to the sky and called out. "Spirit World, hear us. This Cherokee woman we call Little Sparrow is coming to dwell there." They chanted her name over and over for several minutes, an entreaty to the Spirit World.

Catey then took the pot of willow water and placed it next to Amy's body. "This is sacred water," she said to Victoria. "It will cleanse your mama so she can enter into the Spirit World."

The men went outside while Catey and Victoria washed Amy's body and dressed her in her favorite dark blue blouse and a long cotton skirt. Colorful shapes of animals and mythical creatures woven in the fabric stood silent witness to her life. Victoria found her mother's doe skin moccasins and gently placed them on her feet.

When the women finished preparing Amy for burial, Amy called the men back inside the cabin. They wrapped Amy's body in a deer pelt, carried her outside and laid her on the ground beside the grave.

Henri opened the deer pelt and caressed his wife's delicate face one last time with his large, loving hands. He whispered, "*Etre à la paix, mon coeur*. Please be at peace." Then he gently placed a small bowl, two grinding stones and a blanket next to her.

Victoria sobbed as she laid a rabbit pelt and a knife on the blanket. "Mama, I love you."

Jesse placed a small turtle shell on top of the blanket, and Daniel held back tears as he put a small flute, one he had made out of the leg bone of a deer, next to the shell. "Aunt Amy always loved to sing," he whimpered.

Catey carefully laid a small pouch of blue powder next to the rabbit pelt, and Francois added an Indigo blue woven basket.

Henri and Francois lowered Amy's body into the gaping hole that would swallow her forever. When they were finished, both men climbed out of the grave; Henri shivered with grief as Victoria gripped his hand tightly.

Catey lifted her arms and looked to the sky. "Spirit World, Little Sparrow asks to enter. We offer this prayer for her. My grandfather is the fire, my grandmother, the wind. The earth is my mother; the Great Spirit is my father. The world stopped when I was born and laid itself at my feet. At my death, I will swallow the earth whole, and the earth and I will become one."

They filled the grave and placed large rocks over the entire surface to keep animals from digging. Daniel and Jesse plucked several white stones from the stream and used them to build a small pyramid for her marker.

After a few moments of silence, Catey turned to Henri. "The cabin is unclean," she said. "We have to throw out all of the food and burn the bed and blankets."

Henri was stunned. "Do not ask me to do this. Her body is not yet cold. It is our marriage bed."

"Henri, it is the way we have always done. Besides, we don't know what took Amy's life. I've heard talk of villages and towns being wiped out because of some kind with sickness. Do you want to risk that with your family?"

He thought for a moment, and then slowly shook his head. "*Non*. I could not stand to lose another. Tell me what needs to be done."

They set about emptying all the cabinets of food, and Henri broke the bed in small sections and put it in the fireplace. He watched as his life with Amy was reduced to glowing embers. Jesse and Daniel fetched wood in preparation for a new fire. When the fire died, Henri cleaned the hearth and stacked the new wood. Francois helped him build a new bed, and they placed it in the far corner of the cabin.

Henri turned to Catey and asked, "Are we finished?"

Catey shook her head. "No. One more task remains. We are also unclean. Each of us must drink some of the willow water, then we'll wash in it."

After both families completed the cleansing ritual by immersing seven times in the clean, fresh water of the nearby stream, Catey made them supper. They all sat quietly on the porch and picked at their food; no one was really hungry. Victoria helped Catey wash and dry the dishes, and then they joined the men on the porch. No one spoke for what seemed like an eternity.

Finally Catey broke the silence. "Boys, we need to get you home to bed." She hugged Henri and Victoria, then she motioned for her men to follow her back to their cabin. She looked back at Francois, who nodded to her but stayed behind.

"Henri, you and Victoria should come and stay with us tonight," Francois said.

"*Non, frère*. This is our home. We are fine. But thank you."

Francois knew his brother was lying but he could do nothing to help. Amy had been the center of their world, and now she was gone.

Francois stood and hugged Victoria, then went to Henri. He gently pressed his hand on his brother's shoulder, then turned and headed for his home.

The silence was deafening, almost surreal. It was as if the creatures in the forest were also in mourning. Father and daughter sat together on the porch in disbelief at how quickly their world had changed forever. The night's black seemed to engulf them, but for the soft light coming from the small front window of the cabin.

Finally, Victoria looked up at her father. "I suppose we should go to bed, Papa."

"*Oui*, I suppose so." He stood and put his arm around her. "Your mama would not like it if we stayed up all night. She would say we need our rest."

They walked inside the dark cabin, darker now that Amy was gone. Victoria stepped to the ladder that led to her loft bed. She back turned to her father. "Papa, she said she would see me again. Is she really in the Spirit World?" Her eyes pleaded for an answer, and Henri's heart ached.

He searched for the words to console his daughter. "*Oui, ma petite.* I believe she is there now." He knelt down so he could look into her golden eyes and gently held her arms. "And you know I believe she is watching over us, even now. Do you believe this also, *ma cherie*?"

She smiled weakly, nodded and squeezed his neck. "I do, papa...I do."

Chapter 5

Alexander home
Affton, Missouri

Bev walked in the front door. "Man, it's hot out there."

"Yeah, I know," Julie said. "That's why we're doing inside stuff today. We can hit the pool later, if you want."

"Gee, just so happens I brought my suit," Bev laughed. "Where's Michael?"

"He and his dad took the Harleys for a ride. They do it every Sunday after church…weather permitting."

"That's nice. Sort of gets him out of the house for a while. By the way, I saw Ashley and her boyfriend yesterday. What's his name again?"

"Brandon."

"That's right. Gosh, I can't believe it. She's so grown up now. It seems like just last week we were at her baptism"

"I know," Julie said. Her mind flipped back to the church and the ceremony. She could still see the minister lift her only daughter for all to see. "I think I cried more than she did."

"I don't think she cried at all! Do you think she and Brandon will get married?"

"It wouldn't surprise me. He's a nice kid, and he treats her like a queen. But there's been no announcement yet," Julie said.

Bev glanced at the mound of paperwork growing on the dining room table. "So, what's up with the family tree?"

"Well, I thought while Mike's out, we could work on it. For some reason he has been on me about this whole ancestor thing. He thinks it's stupid for me to spend all this time searching for my roots."

"Y'know what I think? I think it's a guy thing, Jules. Most men are just not as interested in this stuff as women are. My theory goes like this – way back when, it was the guys who had to go off and hunt while the women stayed back and took care of the kids and the fire. So it stands to reason that men are always looking forward. They couldn't afford to look back."

"Okay. I'll buy that. But it's his loss."

"Why don't you do it when he's at work?"

"Well, during the summer and when school's out for Christmas and Spring break I do. That's when I go to cemeteries, libraries, that kind of stuff during the week. But when school's in session, he and I only have the weekends. And we spend as much time together as we can. That is when there's not a game or a race on," she laughed.

"Sounds like you have a plan," Bev said. "So what do you need me for?"

"You've done more genealogy than me. I just need your brain. I'm stuck on my great-grandmother and need some advice."

Julie and Bev were best friends. They had been since high school where they met in geometry class. Julie was struggling – Bev wasn't. She took pity on Julie and tutored her. It must have paid off because Julie was voted best geometry teacher in the metro St. Louis area by her Affton High School students last year.

"Well, let's see what you've done so far," Bev said and walked to the table. She noticed an old black fishing tackle box sitting on one of the side chairs. "What's in this?"

Julie grinned. "That's for later."

Bev picked up a folder marked "Mom" and opened it to the first page. "This is just what I expected to see," she said. "I like this form of pedigree. It reminds me of stair steps. Easier to follow than some of the other ones out there.

Julie had written her name in the first step of the pedigree. A line next to her name branched out to the right and became two more steps. Each step contained the names William Baker and Betty Yochem.

"So these are your mom and dad, and you've recorded their birth and death dates and where they were born and where they're buried. That's good." Bev noticed more lines and steps containing the last name of Baker. "It looks like you've been pretty successful with your dad's side."

"Yeah, he was easy. I talked with my uncle Donnie and got a lot of information. Dad's family came from England and I used the Ellis Island web site where I found most of what I need. It's Mom's side where I'm getting frustrated."

"Okay, let's look," Bev said. She gazed down at the pedigree steps. "So your mom's dad, your maternal grandfather, was Robert Yochem. That would be your grandpa Robert you talk about."

"Right."

"And he married Anna Simmons. She was your grandma. And you've got their birth and death dates and where they're buried. Where did you find this stuff?"

"On Familysearch.org," Julie replied. "Have you used it?"

"All the time. It's a great website. That's where I found a lot of my ancestors." Bev refocused on the pedigree steps. "Let's see now, Grandpa Robert's dad, your great-grandpa was named Rogers Yochem and he married a woman named Victoria Levalier. Ooh la la, that sounds French."

"I know. She's the one I'm stuck on. I can't find out much about either of them, or anybody else for that matter. I called my cousin Vicki. She lives up in Eureka Illinois, but she didn't have any information."

"Eureka? I used to work with a woman who went to Eureka College. Did you know it was the first college in Illinois to admit women?"

"No, I didn't."

"That's where President Reagan went to college."

"Uh huh. Mike and I went up there a couple of years ago for a visit and Vicki and her husband, Dick took us on a tour of the campus. If you ever go, stop at the Busy Corner Grill in Goodfield. It's just up the road a bit from Eureka. They have great food. Oh boy, I've got to stop thinking about food."

"You do?"

"It's a long story."

"So is Vicki your only cousin?"

"No. I also e-mailed my cousin, Barbara. She lives in Manito Illinois, just up the road from Eureka. But she didn't have much family history either. It's like all Mom's family just fell off the map."

"Okay. Did your mom ever tell you anything about her grandma and grandpa?" Bev asked.

"You know, I wish I had talked to her more when I was younger. But back then I was more interested in...well, other things," she laughed. "Mom said Victoria was Cherokee Indian. That's an odd name for a Cherokee, don't you think?"

"Yeah, it is. Maybe your cousin Vicki was named after her."

"I asked Vicki that very question. She said she didn't think so since her given name is Vicki, not Victoria. But who knows. Anyway, my mom said she thought Victoria's father was French Canadian, but I can't find anything on that, either. And I have so little information on her husband, the guy named Rogers Yochem. Apparently Victoria and Rogers lived most of their life in Graniteville. That's over in Iron County. Mom said Grandpa Robert was born on their homestead."

"What are we talkin'... 1870's?"

"Yeah, Grandpa Robert was born in 1875. He died before I was born, but Mom said he never talked much about Victoria."

"You never know, he might have been embarrassed that she was Indian."

"I never thought about that. I know I wouldn't be. Ever since I can remember, I've always felt a special bond with Native Americans and nature. Don't ask me why."

"Because you're a certifiable tree hugger, that's why!" Bev laughed.

"Why, thank you. It must be in my DNA. Anyway, the story my mom heard was that Victoria's parents were killed by white men when Victoria was just a little girl, and she was raised by one of the white families. Maybe that's where the English name came from. And Mom told me she remembered that Victoria smoked a corn cob pipe and used to grind corn on a big stone and make corn meal."

"Wait a minute, your mom *knew* Victoria?"

"Yeah, she said they used to go to Graniteville to visit her. I got a copy of Victoria's death certificate from the Ironton court house. She died in 1936."

"Holy crap, Jules. That is so cool," Bev said. "When was she born?"

Julie picked up the manila folder labeled *Mom* and thumbed through the papers until she produced an official-looking document. She placed it on the table in front of Bev. "There is no birth certificate. This is her death certificate. All it says is that she was born in Missouri in 1852. It lists her parents as

Henri Levalier and a woman named Amy. It doesn't show Amy's maiden name."

"So, she was eighty four when she died. Then you know where she's buried."

"Nope," Julie said and pointed to a field on the death certificate. "See, the burial location is blank. I'd love to find her grave and take a picture of the head stone."

"She's probably buried in Graniteville. Have you checked?"

"Yes. The only problem is there's no cemetery in Graniteville. I checked online for cemeteries in the area and the list is huge. I started looking, but decided it would take me forever to check each one of them.

"Well, did the county have any records of them owning land?" Bev jotted notes on the pedigree next to Victoria's name.

"I did find something on that. Rogers had about forty acres of land just outside of Graniteville. He died sometime around 1900. That's it."

"That's a lot. You've been working on this for quite a while, haven't you?"

"Yeah. Off and on for about a year."

"Then what else do you want to find?"

"I don't know. I guess I'm fixated on where she and Rogers are buried. I know where everybody else is buried. If her death certificate listed that, I'd probably feel okay with everything else, but it's just a mystery that I need to solve. I've wracked my brain and I'm coming up empty." Julie popped up from her chair. "Want something to drink? I've got some really good iced tea."

"Yeah, that sounds yummy," Bev replied.

Julie grabbed two glasses from an upper cabinet, and then went to the fridge and pulled out a pitcher of tea. After dropping a couple of ice cubes into each glass, she poured them full and returned to the table.

Bev took a deep drink. "Ooh, that is yummy. Thanks."
Returning to the pedigree, she said, "Well, based on what I've
seen so far, the stuff you've done, I would have done the same
thing. I suggest you go to a meeting of the Genealogical Society.
They meet every month at the library. Somebody there might
have some suggestions. And see what websites are out there on
Cherokee ancestors. There should be something. After all, they
have a big reservation somewhere in Oklahoma. Other than that,
you may have to be satisfied with what you have. Now, I can't
stand it any longer. What's in this old box?"

Julie lifted the box onto the table. "Open it."

Bev reached in and pulled out an old black and white photo.
"Who have we here?"

"It's my grandpa and grandma, Robert and Anna Yochem.
I'm guessing that they're on the front porch of their house, but I
don't know that for sure."

"Neat. Boy, I remember your mom, and now I know where
she got her good looks. Her mother was an attractive woman.
But it looks like she got her high cheek bones from her dad. This
is an important piece of family history. Be sure you scan it and
then put it somewhere safe. But what are these?" she said
referring to a small bundle of papers.

"Read 'em," Julie said.

Bev carefully opened one small, faded sheet and read it. "My
dearest Dutch, I slept so soundly in your arms last night that I
never wanted to wake. You make my life and my world
complete. I love you…Victoria." She looked at Julie. "Dutch?
Whose Dutch?"

Julie shrugged and shook her head. "Don't know. Go ahead,
read another one."

"My darling Victoria, I will work in the field today, but my
mind will be on you. I can't wait to touch your soft skin and look

into your deep eagle eyes. I love you with all my heart…Dutch."
Bev looked at Julie. "These are love letters between Victoria and
somebody named Dutch. Where did you find these?"

"They were in this box in the top of mom's closet when I
cleaned out their house. I guess she forgot they were there."

"But who's Dutch? Maybe a lover? Ooh la la, Victoria. You
little vixen, you."

"Wouldn't it be cool to know for sure?" Julie asked.

"Yeah, it would," Bev replied.

Chapter 6

December 10, 1864
Oregon County, Missouri

Victoria startled awake. Her heart thundered in her chest; her breath came in rapid spurts. She lay still trying to get her bearings. Had she been dreaming? It was so real. She quickly realized that she was lying in her bed; she took a deep breath, threw her legs over the edge and climbed down the ladder from the loft. The soft light from the fire's embers cast long shadows across the tiny cabin. Henri was sitting at the gnarled oak table, bent over his gun.

Victoria squinted. "Papa? It's late. What are you doing? I thought you cleaned that last night."

Henri stopped oiling his rifle and looked up; his brow was deeply furrowed. "Victoria, please go back to bed. You have much to do when morning comes."

"So do you, Papa. But you're doing work you've already done."

She leaned in close to his face and they locked eyes. "You could at least do some of my chores." She was hoping for a smile. He didn't do that much anymore.

He smiled weakly and patted her head. "Why are you up?"

"I had a strange dream."

He laid the rifle down on the table and turned to her. "Do you want to tell me about it?"

She sat in the chair opposite him and yawned. "It was very odd. In my dream I was an eagle and I was flying way up in the sky. I was covered all over with feathers. My wings were strong and they cut through the air like a skinning knife. And I could see everything – everything! There was a tiny little mouse running in the tall grass, and I saw a big black bear pulling a fish out of a stream, and a herd of deer in a field. I was free and felt so powerful, Papa. But then my wings suddenly turned into arms, and I couldn't fly anymore. I started to fall to the ground. The earth kept coming closer and closer. That's when I woke up."

Henri thought a moment and wished, not for the first time, that Amy was there. His only daughter was now twelve, but to him she was still so young. "Your mama would have known the meaning of your dream. I wish she was here now so she could help."

"Well, what do you think it means?" she asked.

"Well, let me think." His eyes wandered to the ceiling. "You are Eagle Eyes, and your eyes are very sharp, even if your wings are broken. You are a strong Cherokee, and you will fly again. But for now you must walk the earth."

Victoria gaped at her father and then she covered her mouth and shook with laughter. "Oh, Papa, that sounded very wise. Are you sure you're not Cherokee, too?" Her eyes twinkled at him, and then turned serious again. "I miss her too. But I feel better now and I'm going back to bed. You should do the same."

He knew his daughter was right; he undressed and reluctantly climbed into the cold, lonely bed. He tried to, but couldn't sleep. *My Little Sparrow, I wish you were here with us.* After a couple of hours, he finally gave up the notion of sleep and got up. The cabin was now cold, so he dressed quickly and stoked the fire. Flames quickly licked up the blackened chimney, and he stood in front of the hearth briefly to warm himself. The fire cracked loudly, and Henri started the coffee and the rest of the day.

He double-checked his leather satchel to make sure he had everything before he donned his fur-lined coat, heavy boots and warm beaver skin cap. He whisked out the cabin door and quickly returned with a large stack of clean, dry logs. He then climbed the ladder to the loft where Victoria lay sleeping. Just as he reached to touch her shoulder, he realized he was looking at her feet. He shook his head and moved to the foot of the bed. *Oh child, you are such a little character.* He gently stroked her head. "Victoria."

"Yes, Papa," she answered sleepily and slowly opened her eyes.

"I am leaving now and will be gone for a while. But I will be back by dark. I put more wood on the fire. It is cold outside."

She was awake now and looked up at him. "But, I want to go with you. You may need help with the traps."

"Not today, *ma fille douce*. We discussed this already. It is cold and I need you here to keep the fire alive so I can warm up quickly when I return."

"I know, Papa. But you would finish faster if I help. Maybe you should just stay here today and go tomorrow."

"I only put out a few traps, down by the river. Just enough for us to have some meat. You do like meat don't you?"

"Yes, I like meat," she giggled.

"Besides, it will be cold tomorrow, too, *non*? We do what we must. I will be back by nightfall."

"Do you have your necklace?" she asked.

"I am wearing it, see." A dark, leather strap hung around his neck. On it dangled a single claw taken from a cougar he killed earlier in the summer. Cougars were rare in the mountains these days, and Henri didn't want to kill it, but he surprised the big cat while it was eating – the wrong thing to do. It was kill or be killed. Both he and Victoria now considered it a good luck charm.

"It will keep me safe. It always does. Now, give me a hug." He bent down and kissed her forehead, and she hugged him tightly. She breathed in the musky scent that flowed out from his deerskin jacket; she didn't want to let go.

He paused, looked at her nodded. *"Ne pas craindre quel est pour venir. L'embrasser."*

"I will, Papa."

She took comfort in his words, and believed them to be true. From under her blanket, she watched him pick up his rifle and step out into the frigid morning, then she snuggled back down into the warmth. It was still cold in the cabin and she wanted to wait until the fire warmed it.

She had her chores finished before midday and it had warmed up a little outside. The fire didn't require as much stoking now.

"Well, Mama, I think I'll surprise Papa with some stew. It's his favorite. What do you think?" She liked talking to her mother; sometimes, when it was very quiet, she actually thought she heard her reply.

It was the last of the meat, but Henri was a good trapper. Even though the hills contained fewer animals now, they never went without. She sang as she chopped carrots, wild onions and potatoes to add to the brew of dried meat and spices. Soon the concoction was bubbling its own happy tune.

Her final task was to hone her skinning knife; eight inches of razor sharp steel always cut a perfect pelt. By the time she finished, the sun was setting lower in the sky. She held the knife up; the blade gleamed in the firelight. "What do you think Mama? I think it's ready."

The stew smelled good. "Tell Papa to hurry. I'm getting hungry," she giggled.

Just then Victoria heard footsteps near the front of the cabin. "Hey!" someone called out. "Anybody in there?"

She didn't recognize the deep voice coming from outside. She picked up her knife and cautiously opened the front door. A man holding a long rifle and shouldering a large cotton bag stood near the porch. His mouth smiled, but his eyes didn't. His shoulder-length hair and long, shaggy beard were as matted as his clothes, and her nose told her that he was in desperate need of a bath.

"Afternoon, ma'am. I'm…uh…lookin' fer work. Was wonderin' if y'all needed an extry hand?"

Her heart thundered, but she had been taught to show no fear. She stood boldly in the doorway; her hand gripped the skinning knife. She said, "I'm sorry, but we don't need any help."

"You and yer family do alright then?" the stranger asked as he tried to peer around her into the cabin.

"Yes, we do alright."

"Yer husband, he around?"

"No, but my papa is out back. He'll be here very soon." She locked her knees to keep them from trembling. *Papa, please hurry!*

The stranger plopped the bag down heavily on the ground. "Lordy, somethin' sure smells good. Do ya think y'all could spare a bite for a hungry man?" His eyes narrowed.

"Wait here," she said. She stepped inside and closed and bolted the door. "Help me, Mama," she whispered.

She slipped the knife into her belt sheath and quickly ladled some stew into an old bowl. She stepped out and placed the bowl on the porch.

"That's all we have. And I say again, we have no work."

"Victoria, who is that with you?" Francois called, approaching the cabin.

She breathed a sigh of relief. "This man...he's looking for work and was hungry. I told him we have no work."

Francois looked at the stranger; he didn't like what he saw. He stepped onto the porch and stood slightly in front of Victoria. She rested her hand on her knife.

Disappointed at the interruption - Francois was taller and appeared to be much stronger - the stranger hungrily ate the stew and wiped his mouth with his sleeve. "That was mighty tasty. Much obliged." He grinned, exposing gnarly teeth through his long, unkempt mustache. Victoria leaned out from behind Francois and glared at the stranger.

"Y'all don't know where I might find a bed fer the night?"

"There is a town. It is five miles to the north. They have beds there. Just follow the trail over there," Francois nodded towards the forest but didn't take his eyes off the man.

"Well, then I guess I'll be movin' that way. Y'all have a nice evenin'."

They watched him skulk away toward the dense forest. He turned and leered back at them, and then he was gone.

"How long was he here?" Francois asked.

"Only a few minutes before you came," Victoria said and hugged him. "He scared me."

"I was down by the stream and suddenly got a strange feeling that something was wrong so I rushed here. Thank goodness I did. I do not like him, Victoria. I feel he is no good. We must take heed to watch for his return," Francois said. "Where is your papa?"

"He isn't back yet. He said he would be back by dark, and it's getting late."

He looked into her frightened eyes. "Maybe his traps were empty and he found some good trails and decided to do a little hunting. We should not worry. He will be fine. I think he is sitting by a warm fire right now chewing on an old rabbit." He hoped his smile was convincing though he still couldn't shake the feeling of dread. "If he is not back by daylight, we will go to hunt and find him. Why don't you come and have supper with us?"

"No, I'll stay and wait. He'll be hungry when he gets here."

She picked at the stew. *Papa, where are you?* Later that evening Francois stopped by to check on her, the encounter with the suspicious stranger still fresh in his memory.

"He is not back yet? Wait till I see him. I thought I heard a shot a while ago. How dare he go hunting without me! Catey says you should stay with us tonight."

"No. I want to be here when he comes home."

"Then I will stay with you. Okay? You get some sleep. I will keep the fire hot."

She slept fitfully, wakened by the slightest sound. Visions of the stranger with the hate-filled eyes haunted her dreams.

Dawn crept into the tiny cabin and Henri had not returned. They dressed quickly and stepped out into the frigid air. Francois shivered.

"Do you know where he was going?" he asked.

"He went to check his traps down by the river, near the rock creek," Victoria replied.

"Then that is where we will go."

The snow that had fallen the previous night was melting; the thawed earth was now a blanket of mud. By mid morning they were close to the river.

"Henri! Henri! Are you here?" Francois called, but the forest was silent. "Maybe he set up camp by the river."

The two searchers made their way down a steep embankment, grasping small trees and straddling fallen logs, slipping and tumbling in the wet, muddy snow. They found one of Henri's empty traps near the water's edge.

"He was here," Francois said.

Victoria looked in the sand. "Uncle," she said pointing to two sets of footprints headed downstream.

"Two sets?" Concern crept into his voice, and they quickly began to follow the trail.

Victoria stopped briefly to scan the area, desperately looking for her father. Francois continued ahead, his eyes on the footprints. Suddenly she saw it - her father's good luck necklace. It was almost completely buried in the sand, the tip of the cougar claw barely visible. She pulled it out of the muck, rubbed off some of the sand, and put it in her pocket. Just ahead, Francois had also stopped. Thirty yards downstream something in the shallow part of the river had caught his eye.

"Oh, *mon Dieu*!" He gasped and grabbed Victoria's arm. They rushed toward the river.

Then she saw him. "Papa!" she screamed and flailed into the water. She didn't feel the icy splash on her arms and face as she desperately tried to pull her father's body from the river. Tears streamed down her face and she frantically tugged at his coat. "No! Papa! No!"

Henri's massive right hand, now stiff with death, gripped an empty trap. They dragged his body to the sandy river bank, held each other and cried.

"Who would do this?" she sobbed. "Who?"

"It has no meaning. Whoever did this...wait, where is his rifle? Did he take his gun with him?"

"He always takes it," she said.

Francois began to read the footprints in the sand. "Look. He was checking his traps. Someone followed him. They both stopped."

Victoria stared at the impressions. "But Papa didn't turn around. The killer shot him...in the back. He must have taken Papa's rifle and ran away. Coward!" she screamed, her voice echoed in the snow-covered hills. A single set of footprints led downstream for a few yards and then disappeared into the river.

Francois' chin stiffened. He gripped Victoria's shoulders and looked squarely at her. "Now listen to me. We must take your papa home. I will come back and try to find the monster that did this."

"I'll help you."

"*Non*. It is too dangerous!"

"My papa is dead! I'm coming with you!" she sobbed defiantly.

She was an expert tracker and deft with a skinning knife. His eyes softened. "All right, you and me, we will track him, but first we must get your papa home. We will make a litter. Cut some of those birch limbs. Make sure they are big and strong. I will strip the bark so we can tie the limbs together."

Neither spoke during the long, grueling task of building a litter to transport Henri's body. Victoria was in shock, but Francois was planning the hunt.

It was almost dark by the time they reached home. Francois burst into the cabin and stood motionless, staring at his wife.

"Did you find him?" Catey asked anxiously. She saw the anger and sadness in his eyes. "What's happened?"

"Catey, my brother is dead."

She shrank back, speechless, her eyes wide with shock.

"He was murdered! A coward shot him in the back. We will bury him in the morning. Then Victoria and I will go back to track down the killer." He looked toward the north. *I know who I'm looking for.*

Daniel and Jesse helped Francois dig up the partially frozen earth next to Amy's grave. Victoria knelt down to see her father for the last time. She clutched his leather necklace in her trembling hands. "When he wore it, he was safe. But without it..."

Francois lifted the necklace from her grasp, retied the leather straps and placed it over her head. "It is a powerful necklace. It kept him safe from the wild animals, Victoria. But it could not save him from the two-legged kind. He is with your mama now."

They gathered stones from the stream and, like they did with Amy, made a pyramid to mark his grave. When they were finished, Francois looked toward the sky. "Henri, my brother, be at rest eternal. We will find who did this and they will pay dearly."

"I should have been with him, Uncle. I could have saved him," Victoria cried.

"*Non*, Victoria. You would have been killed, too. Some people, they kill for the smallest of reasons, they do not care. Do not blame yourself."

Catey held Victoria's hands. "Won't you come and live with us, Victoria?"

Victoria shook her head. "No, Aunt Catey. I want to stay here. This is my home."

"If only for the winter. Then come back here in the spring. Please come with us so we know you will be safe," Catey pleaded.

Victoria didn't have the strength to argue. "For the winter...after we find the man who killed Papa."

Chapter 7

Alexander home
Affton, Missouri

Early Monday morning Julie and Mike finished loading the bus with clothes, groceries, and a case each of beer and bottled water. It wasn't really a bus, but a motor home they bought after Chris graduated from tech school.

"Matt says Rachel knows some really neat hiking trails we can take."

"We?" Mike asked.

"Yeah, Rachel and me. You can stay back and hold down the fort with Matt."

"Hey, steaks, stogies, beer and Matt…now that's what I call camping."

Mike filled the fresh water tank, made sure the propane level was sufficient, and checked the air pressure in the tires.

"Got your cell phone?"

"Yes, dear, it's on. I'll call you when I get there. Love you."

"Love you, too," he said with a hug and kiss. "See you Friday."

The three hundred fifty horsepower Caterpillar diesel engine roared to life, settled into a deep pulsing growl and waited for Julie to step on the accelerator. She kept an eye on the traffic; the bus was big, and she wanted a safety cushion between it and the other cars around her.

Her route took her past the Oakland House, a popular tourist attraction she and Ashley toured a few months back. Ashley wanted to see it for its architecture; Julie thought it would make a nice setting for a wedding and a reception. The brochure said the ornate limestone mansion was built in the 1800's, and was owned by Louis Benoist, son of a French Canadian fur trader. Louis opted for something other than the fur trade and became a well-known banker in the Affton area. It was then that Julie realized French Canadians lived and worked in the area about the time Victoria was born. Maybe the story of Henri Levalier was true after all.

She traveled down Highway 30, also known as Gravois Road, and eased past Grant's Farm, home of the Anheuser Busch Clydesdale horses. She glanced over and saw several of the gentle giants grazing out in the pasture, their bobbed tails whisked across their huge rear ends in an attempt to keep the flies away.

"I know I need to lose weight, but I hope my butt's not that big," she said.

Grant's Farm was more than just a horse farm. She remembered how the kids squealed with delight when she and Mike took them on their first tram ride through Deer Park on the grounds. North American bison, African zebras and European antelope were among the hundreds of animals that roamed the area. The price was right - free admission, and two free beers. She liked the admission – Mike liked the beers.

She took Interstate 270 to I55 south, then Highway H at the town of Festus, and finally to Highway 21. She could have driven the new Highway 21, its four lanes moved traffic along faster, but today she wasn't in a hurry. The map identified Highway 21 as a scenic route. Julie liked to call it Mother Nature's yellow brick road, its narrow path gently curved through the rolling Missouri hills and skirted the outer edge of one of the many areas designated as the Mark Twain National Forest. The forest, named after the author, dotted the southern half of Missouri with nine different forested areas. Oregon County, where Julie was headed, boasted over a hundred thousand acres of it.

Today's meander in the wilderness was exceptional. Thousands of wildflowers, among them red clover, wild plum, pink prairie rose and blue morning glory, lined both sides of the narrow, two lane winding road, each wanting to share its own seductive scent with the world. Julie never wore perfume; most were too phony for her. She took a deep breath. *Wow! Now I could wear this. Too bad nobody can copy it.*

The massive oaks, pines, and maples – trees that had been growing in the area for hundreds of years – blanketed the sky with their leaves and blocked the sun's harsh rays; the inside of the bus remained relatively cool. But Julie had also traveled this road in the fall when those same leaves became a stunning quilt of color. Brilliant reds, deep oranges, bright yellows and dark muted browns never ceased to leave her breathless. She loved this forest – regardless of the season.

She drove past small, progressive bergs with names like Fertile, Old Mines, Potosi, Caledonia, and Belleview. Houses along the route ran the gamut, from small trailers whose front yards were choked with old, rusty cars and bent bicycles, to large, multi-story eye poppers with their perfectly manicured, uninteresting, sterile-looking lawns.

Just outside the town of Pilot Knob she stopped at a picnic area to stretch her legs. A sign advertising the nearby Fort Davidson State Historic Site shimmered on a fence post. *Maybe we should go there someday. It might be interesting. Mike likes all that army stuff – soldiers and big guns.*

Near Doniphan she turned on to Highway 160, crossed over the Current River and drove the final twenty-five miles to Big Forest Campground just outside of Riverton Missouri. She and Mike liked this place. Located near the Eleven Point River, the campground had full hook-up spaces for two hundred recreational vehicles, as well as several primitive sites for tent campers. Amenities at the park included a pool, a play area for the kids, laundry facilities, two volleyball and shuffleboard courts, and a recreation hall for indoor activities. Several freshly painted picnic tables and a large open grill huddled under a roofed pavilion, a location that came in handy when campers wanted to picnic on a rainy day.

Some came to relax or to fish, some to canoe or kayak the Eleven Point. Still others sought out Big Forest to hike the elaborate trails that snaked through the woods, affectionately know to the locals as The Wilderness. Beginners could walk one fairly flat, well-trodden path three miles in length. More advanced hikers enjoyed the intermediate routes. Extreme hikers packed tents and overnight supplies when they tackled the steep, rocky terrain of the advanced trails. GPS tracking devices, or as Matt and Rachel called them, hiker finders, were a must. Many a seasoned hiker owed their life to the cell phone-sized unit that sent signals out to pinpoint their location to rescuers.

Julie turned the bus into the campground and eased it up next to a sign that read *STOP HERE TO REGISTER*. She put the coach in park, shut off the engine and stepped out onto the steamy, hot blacktop drive. The smell, something akin to hot tar, like the kind they use to repair roofs, assaulted her nose. *Yuck. Matt lied. It's hot here, too!*

The air conditioned campground office was a welcome relief from the oppressive heat. It was small, but neat and orderly. A white chalkboard map hung on the opposite wall and showed the locations of the pool, laundry, showers and restrooms, a trash dumpster and each numbered camp site.

Reserved sites contained guest's names printed in black dry erase marker with arrival and departure dates noted in red. Julie looked for their name and found it. Matt's name was written in the spot next to hers. Not all of the spaces were occupied, but it was only Monday. Summer was peak time for camping and Julie guessed the park would be full by Friday evening.

A woman clad in khaki Capri pants and a bright yellow V-neck top was seated at a small gray desk behind the counter. She looked up from her computer. "Hello, can I help you?" Her twinkling eyes and broad smile made Julie feel at ease immediately.

"We have reservations for Alexander."

"Of course, let me pull you up," she said. Her slender fingers deftly tapped the computer keys. "Here we are. Michael and Julie. Staying till Sunday?"

"Yes. My brother and his wife are coming here, too. Matt and Rachel Baker."

"Oh, the Baker's are already here. They came in about ten o'clock this morning. You'll be parked next to them on space twelve. That's on Robin's Nest Lane."

"Great. Thank you. You know, my brother lied to me. It's hot here too."

"Yes, it is. But the river's nice and cool. Are you going canoeing?"

"No, my sister-in-law and I are going to try our hand at the hiking trails."

"Oh, you'll have a good time. I've walked a little bit on my days off. It was fun. By the way, I'm Donna O'Neal. You obviously are Julie," she laughed.

"You got it. Nice to meet you, Donna. You're new at the office, aren't you?

"Yes, my husband and I are full-timers. We took this job in the spring and we'll be here through the summer. Phil gets antsy when we stay in one place too long. And he hates the cold weather. We'll probably head somewhere warm for the winter."

"You sound like my husband," Julie said. "He must have been a nomad in a previous life. I don't think he would have any problem selling the house and living full time in the motor home. Traveling is fun, but I need to have roots."

Donna nodded. "I understand. Full-timing isn't for everybody. But we're what you call worker-campers and that has its perks. You know, free lot rent for as long as we work here."

"That's a good tradeoff. The campground owners get someone to work, basically for free."

"Well, we do get a small salary. It helps pay for groceries."

"Gotta eat."

"Sometimes I wish we didn't have to! Well, enough about food. Let's get you registered so you can start enjoying your stay."

Julie paid for the week and picked up a listing of all the activities available in the park for the month. Campers could enjoy dance lessons, water aerobics, group fishing and canoe trips, bingo, and other forms of entertainment - or they could just kick back and relax.

A nondenominational church service was held on Sunday mornings in the recreation hall. Sunday afternoon was the usual ice cream social where for two dollars you could get two huge scoops of vanilla ice cream and then overdose on toppings like chocolate syrup, nuts, whipped cream, strawberries, coconut, chocolate chips. It was always a big hit with the seniors or families with kids - lots of bang for the buck.

"My son will escort you to your site," Donna said. "Eric...Eric!" A young man stepped into the office. Julie guessed him to be in his early twenties.

"Yeah...mom," he said.

"Eric, please take Mrs. Alexander to site twelve at Robin's Nest Lane. Got that? Robin's Nest Lane. Site number twelve, okay?"

"Robin's Nest. Site...twelve. Got it, Mom," Eric repeated.

Julie smiled and extended her hand. "Hi, I'm Julie."

"Hi...Julie. I'm...Eric." His handshake was soft, almost limp, and Julie suspected Eric might be mentally challenged.

Donna reassured her. "He'll take good care of you."

"Thanks. See you later. Stay cool."

They walked out into the oppressive heat, and Eric climbed into a nearby golf cart. "Now...just follow me," he called out.

Julie fired up the bus and edged in behind Eric. He drove slowly at first. Then when he glanced back and saw that she was right behind him, he picked up the pace. They turned right on Cardinal Drive, then left onto Robin's Nest Lane, where Julie saw Matt's blue and white fifth wheel camper parked on spot fourteen.

Eric pointed to the number twelve posted on a large wooden stake. Julie tapped on her horn and waved. He waved back, then turned his golf cart around and headed back to the office.

Matt was lazing in his recliner under the camper's awning when she pulled up. "Rachel, she's here," he called, then he sprang up and helped guide Julie back into her site. She stepped out of the bus and was greeted with hugs and kisses.

"Before I do anything else, let me call home," Julie said.

"Okay, then we'll help you set up," Matt replied.

Mike was relieved to hear her voice. "Glad you made it safe. I'll see you Friday, hon," he said.

"I'll check in with you before then. Matt and Rachel are helping me set up."

She hung up and called out. "Okay, ready when you guys are."

"I've got the back," Matt replied. He walked to the rear of the bus and opened the basement door exposing the power cord, water hose and flexible sewer hose. He plugged the cord into an electric outlet that was attached to a nearby four by four post, screwed the water hose to the outside faucet and inserted the sewer hose into a nearby PVC pipe; this would serve as a connection to the park's septic system.

Inside, Julie pressed the *OUT* button next to the driver's seat and extended the slides on either side of the living room area. Now, instead of feeling cramped in a tight space, she could stretch out in a twelve by twelve living room/kitchen. She went outside and helped Rachel roll out the exterior awning and secure it. Though most of the sites were shaded by large oak and maple trees, it never hurt to have the awning out - just in case a stray shower happened or a few unwanted bugs or bird droppings decided to drop in from the overhanging tree limbs. Finally, Julie opened one of the basement doors on the bus and took out the lawn chairs, folding table and charcoal grill and put them on the concrete patio.

"Thanks guys," Julie said.

"No problem, sis," Matt replied.

"Okay, Matt said you wanted to burn some calories. Ready for that hike?" Rachel asked.

"So soon? Yeah, why not? Let me get my stuff. Can we walk through the rest of the park before we go?"

"Sure. That's a good way to warm up those leg muscles before the big hike."

"Terrific," Julie groaned.

"I'm stayin' right here in the shade. You two go on," Matt said and settled into one of the canvas recliners with a cold glass of iced tea.

"What? Too hot for ya?" Julie laughed.

"Oh, just go on your hike. And take the hiker finders with you," Matt said.

Julie turned to Rachel. "I suppose you've already had your walk around the park."

"Well, yeah, but it's been a couple of hours. Maybe more campers have come in."

They walked out to Robin's Nest Lane where Rachel pointed to the two motor homes parked directly across the street. "First off, our neighbors over there are the Maynard's, John and Rose. They're full-timers. They sold their cattle ranch in Wyoming last year for big bucks and decided to see the country. She loves to bake and wants to share with everyone, so I hope you can resist her tasty temptations."

"Oh, that's just great. You know that's my downfall. On my way down here I made a plan. I've decided to swear off sweets until I lose this fat."

"You don't need to swear off all of them. Just cut back on your portion size," Rachel said.

"Okay, I'm assigning you to be my food manager."

"Done!"

"So, what's behind door number two?"

"That would be Stan and Lois. I think their last name is Yates. He runs a hunting and fishing guide service over near

Thomas Pass. They're here for a couple of days so he can drum up some business. They seem nice. She's pretty quiet, though."

"Is there a door number three?"

"Yep, comin' right up."

The next six sites were vacant, and the two women continued down the lane to a small pop-up camper. A couple was lounging under a large oak tree in matching reclining chairs.

"Thought you were goin' fishin'," Rachel called out.

"Ya know what they say, the big ones sleep in late. We'll wait till after lunch. Then hit 'em hard," the man replied.

"This is my sister-in-law, Julie. She's here for the week."

The couple waved. "Hi Julie."

Julie waved back. "Good luck fishing."

Rachel continued. "That's Tom and Carolyn Pettyjohn. They're from Iowa somewhere. They love to fish and know Stan and Lois back there."

"I'm impressed. How is it you know so much about everyone?"

"Must rub off from Matt," Rachel grinned.

Their walk took them past a small travel trailer on space number forty. Nestled near a row of tall maples, it appeared to be vacant, ready for the junk yard.

"What's up with *this* thing?" Julie asked.

"Don't have a clue. What a dump, huh?"

"Uh…does anybody even stay there?"

"Your guess is as good as mine. But check out the old car parked on the side. I'd hate to see what comes out of that."

The trailer was small, Julie guessed only about twenty four feet long. The exterior appeared at one time to be bright white, but now shimmered a soft green thanks to years of mildew and neglect. Ham radio and CB antennas spiked up from the roof, and the front lawn was sprinkled with several broken lawn chairs, an old bicycle and a rusty gas grill.

"Looks like a poor excuse for a bad yard sale," Julie said.

"Yeah, we'll have to get the scoop on that one. Come on, let's get moving."

They turned the corner and walked down Sparrow Street.

"Okay, how about this one?" Julie asked looking at a small mini van parked on site four.

"Wait till you see this guy," Rachel whispered. "His name is Howard and he lives with his girlfriend, Sheila. She told me they met at a truck stop on I40 somewhere in Oklahoma. They travel around the country and live in that thing. He takes odd jobs and doesn't stay in one place very long. I think the IRS must be on his tail. Or the mob."

"Or an ex wife."

"Too funny. Well, those are the only ones I know about so far."

"Pretty impressive."

"Yeah, but there are so many stories, so little time."

"Are these the hiking trails?" Julie asked.

"Yep," Rachel said. "I can't believe in all the times you guys have been here that you didn't know about these." A large map posted next to the trail head detailed five different ones. Colors identified the degree of severity - one green trail for beginners, two yellow ones for the more advanced hikers and two red trails for extreme hikers.

"Hiking was not high on my priority list. It still isn't. When Mike and I come here it's to relax and enjoy the down-time," Julie said.

Rachel said, "Well, let's see if we can't change those priorities, huh? I usually take the yellow trails. Matt's more adventurous than I am. He took a red trail once. He had to register with the office and give them a time when he expected to be back. That way if he didn't show up, someone in the office would call the search and rescue team. Serious stuff."

"Uh, I may be old enough for the Red Hat Society, but I'm not into red today," Julie said.

"Well, which color?" Rachel asked.

"Let's try a yellow one. I'm gonna consider myself in the more advanced group."

Rachel smiled. "Okay, which one?"

Julie studied the map carefully. "How 'bout this one," she said. "It looks like it goes next to the river."

"What are we waitin' for? Let's do it."

Chapter 8

December, 1864
Oregon County, Missouri

Francois and Victoria stood at the spot where they had found Henri's body. The day was cold, the air crisp and fresh. On any other day like this, she would be hunting and trapping with her father. But today she was going to be hunting and trapping another kind of animal.

"The footprints lead into the stream. Let's go see if he came out on the other side," Francois said.

The icy water sent chills up her spine. "I don't see anything," she said as she combed the sandy banks.

"That means he walked in the water for some time and then got out. But he could not stay in it very long. It would freeze him. We will go downstream and look on both sides. If we do not find his tracks, we will come back upstream. We will find him," Francois said.

Victoria shook her head. "Uncle, we should split up. We can track him faster if you go one way and I go another way."

Francois shot back angrily. "*Non*! You will not go by yourself. This man killed your papa, Victoria. He could kill you, too."

She glared at him. "You say that I'm the best tracker you ever saw. Isn't that right?"

"That is not important right now."

"Yes, it is!" she insisted. "We're both good trackers. So, if we separate we can cover more ground. Whoever finds him, tie him up and yell out. And if we don't find him, we meet at the place where the stream meets the river. Time is wasting, Uncle."

Francois saw the determination in her eyes, those pale golden eyes of her mother. He would never forgive himself if something happened to her, but he knew she was right.

"All right, but you must take my pistol. I have my rifle. If you find him, do not kill him. Understand? Just tie him up. Shoot the gun in the air. I will hear it and find you. And if I find him, I will fire my rifle, and you find me."

Victoria's eyes widened with anticipation. "We can do this, Uncle."

Francois removed his holster and strapped it around Victoria's waist; it hung low on her hip. "I think it is too heavy for you."

"No. It isn't. We have to hurry."

He took her forearms in his hands and looked deep into her eyes. "Now, you go up the stream and I will go down to where the stream meets the river. He is a killer, Eagle Eyes. *Faire attention*!"

"I'll be careful, Uncle."

She walked in the shallow, icy water looking for any sign of a killer; the heavy pistol bounced on her hip. Though still struggling with the loss of her father, she knew she had to focus her energy on the search. Once they found Henri's murderer, she would find time to grieve. She noted a deer trail on one side of the bank, but no sign of a human anywhere.

"He had to come this way. He *had* to. Oh, Papa, let me find him," she whispered.

She sloshed along for another half hour, moving from one side of the stream to the other. Nothing. The sun hung low in the winter sky; it didn't offer much warmth. Her toes and fingers were numb, her teeth chattered, and her lungs ached from the frigid air.

She stopped to blow into her hands when suddenly she saw them, coming out of the water and onto the sandy bank. They were headed for the deep woods. And it looked like he was dragging something behind him...dead animals from Henri's traps. She wasn't cold anymore; now she was the eagle who walked. She quickened her pace; her heart pounded wildly. She smiled when she saw broken branches on several briar bushes and a small piece of cloth hanging from a long, sharp thorn. *If you're the one I'm looking for, I hope it hurt.* She silently followed the trail for the rest of the afternoon. Toward sunset she saw a thin trail of smoke rising up from a nearby glade. Her body shook with excitement. *Do not fear what is to come. Embrace it!*

Chapter 9

Big Forest Campground
Riverton, Missouri

"Okay, I'm ready. Let's go," Julie said.

The narrow path was lined with thick briar bushes and small trees, and quickly sloped at a slight incline. They weaved their way toward a small stream, avoiding the sharp thorns and softball-sized rocks and exposed tree roots erupting from the path.

"Man, am I glad we took an *easy* one," Julie puffed. Her leg muscles burned and sweat drizzled down her back, soaking her shirt. She suddenly realized just how out of shape she was. They stopped briefly at the bottom of the hill.

"Need a rest?" Rachel asked.

"No, what's that saying about no pain, no gain? I'll be fine."

The two followed the stream for about ten minutes, then splashed through it and started up the opposite bank. The water was clear and cold; it felt good on a hot afternoon. They paused several times so Julie could catch her breath. At one stop, Julie was surprised to see several small, round thorn bushes covered with tiny purple flowers.

She pointed to the flowers and said, "These things remind me of Mom's old swim cap. She wore it once when we she and Dad went canoeing with Mike and me on the Current River."

"A swim cap? On the Current?" Rachel said.

"I know. But she insisted on wearing that hideous thing. Said she didn't want to get her hair wet. Know what I think?"

"What?"

"I think she just wanted people to notice a sixty-five year-old woman in a canoe paddling downstream. She had a blast that day." Julie smiled, remembering the joy on her mother's face.

"Sixty-five isn't old," Rachel said.

"Yeah, I know. I miss her. That's why I'm here today. I need to get these old bones stronger." She took a deep breath. "Look around, Rachel. Isn't this remarkable?"

"Yes, it is. You know, I have to admit, I've walked these paths lots of times, but never really appreciated the beauty here," Rachel said.

"See, there's more to life than burning calories."

"Okay, tree hugger. Point taken. Come on. Let's see what else we can find."

They walked for another thirty minutes, climbing over fallen, moss-covered trees, snaking around bushes and stooping to dodge low hanging tree branches. Deep in the forest it was dark and cool.

"Maybe we should just camp here," Julie laughed.

"Yeah, leave Matt in the heat," Rachel said.

Sparrows, blue jays and a bright red cardinal flitted from branch to branch in the majestic maples. Their squawking seemed to be warning the other forest residents that intruders were near.

Julie knelt down and put her hand on the dirt path. "Look at the size of this paw print. It looks like a big critter was here, maybe a dog or a coyote. We'd better be on the lookout."

"How is it you see this stuff?" Rachel asked. "I would never have noticed it."

"I don't know. I just do."

"Well, remind me never to try and hide anything from you. Are you sure you don't have bionic eyes?"

"Not bad for an old hag, huh?"

The path wound around and eventually re-emerged near the stream; a flat section of bank beckoned. "Looks like a good spot to park it," Rachel remarked. They plopped down on the cool, sandy bank and drank from their water bottles.

"Want part of my protein bar?" Rachel asked.

"Sure. I didn't eat lunch and I could use something," Julie said.

They munched on the chewy granola and almonds and sat immersed in an area where time seemed to stand still.

"Just imagine," Julie said. "This area hasn't changed in hundreds, maybe thousands of years. Makes you realize how insignificant you really are. We'll be gone in fifty years, but this forest will still be here."

Rachel replied. "Yep. It's really old. Speaking of old…be sure to take some ibuprofen when you get back."

"Don't worry, my legs will remind me. And I'm not old! I'm an Amazon!"

"A what?"

"An Amazon. You know, Amazon women were strong and powerful. My old gym teacher used to call me that."

"Wasn't that a B movie way back in the 60's?"

"I think you're right. But, since you're so young, how would you know that?"

"Matt told me."

They watched the water ripple over several large stones jutting out of the middle of the stream; the sound was soft, soothing.

Julie sniffed the air. "Smell that?"

"What?" Rachel asked.

"It smells like dirt."

"Well, duh, Einstein. We're sittin' in it."

Julie rolled her eyes. "But this is a different dirt smell. It's coming from the wet rocks in the stream." Something about the minerals that make up the rocks combining with the water. When they get wet, they smell like that. Kinda like dirt."

"If you say so, tree hugger."

Suddenly Julie was aware of an overwhelming feeling, as if being cradled in loving arms. She sat back against the bank and let her mind absorb the moment. It was as if she belonged there.

"This is kinda like heaven, don't you think?"

"I guess. Ready to go? We should probably get back."

"Ready."

When Julie turned toward the trail she spotted something over her right shoulder next to a large pine tree. "Hey, check this out. Looks like some kind of marker."

"Again with the bionic eyes!" Rachel said.

They looked down at two small mounds of white stones stacked about six inches high and separated by about two feet. They were almost concealed by the tall grass.

"A path marker?" Rachel suggested. "Weird though, almost looks like the ground has boobs." Both women laughed. "I think they've been here a long time. Wonder if they're grave markers?"

"Out here? Why would they be out here? There aren't any houses here," Julie said.

"Yeah, but that doesn't mean there weren't at one time."

"I don't know. I guess they could be if they're that old," Julie said.

They stowed their water bottles and continued down the path for another thirty minutes until they saw the campground. "Eureka!" Julie yelled.

"What? You're tired? I thought we'd turn around and go back," Rachel said.

"No way, Josephine! My butt's ready for that lounge chair."

"Well, for a beginner, you did good today. We'll try the other path tomorrow, if you're not too sore."

"Don't worry, this Amazon will be ready."

Matt was napping in his lounge chair.

"Hey! Detective!" Rachel yelled.

He slowly opened one eye. "What? You guys back so soon? What time is it?" He glanced at his watch. "Holy schmolly, it's four o'clock. That was a long hike for you two. Another hour and I'd be out looking for ya."

"Yeah, right," Rachel laughed. "You cookin' dinner?"

Matt sat up in his chair. "Sure. How do grilled chicken breasts and a salad sound?"

"Sounds great," both replied.

"I brought chicken, too. Want to use mine?" Julie asked.

"Nah. Save yours for tomorrow. I'll start the coals."

"I need a shower. See you guys in a bit," Julie said. She stood under the hot pulsing jets, letting them work on her aching muscles. She realized that the doctor was right...she did need to get in better shape.

While drying her hair, she let her mind wander back to the hiking trail. She could still hear the water from the stream and smell the damp forest floor. The experience had heightened her senses, made her feel rejuvenated, and she couldn't wait to take tomorrow's trail. After downing two ibuprofen capsules, she wandered over to her brother's camper.

She plopped down in the canvas recliner. "I feel better now!"

"You smell better, too," Matt said. "How about a glass of wine?"

"Sure."

"Officer Matt here has the 4-1-1 on the new arrivals," Rachel said sipping her Chardonnay.

"Well, let's hear it."

Matt pointed out a blue motor home. "See that camper down at the corner of Robin's Nest & Sparrow? The guy was having trouble backing in, so I want down to help him out. His name is Hal Evans. Wife is Harriet. They're from Indiana. She's nice. He's kinda weird."

"Matt calls him Mr. Security," Rachel said.

"Yeah, it's funny. He got out of the rig and locked it, introduced himself and his wife, thanked me, then unlocked the coach and went back inside to lower the leveling jacks. I thought that was kinda odd, so I stayed around a few more minutes to be sure they didn't need any more help. He came back outside and locked the door…again. Then, before he hooked up power and everything else, he walked around the coach and jiggled each door handle on the basement compartments and on his tow car. Then, get this…he did the same thing all over again. I'd seen enough. I got outa there."

"I believe that's called obsessive compulsive behavior," Julie said.

"I'll say obsessive compulsive. Oh, and then wait till you see this huge bus over on Bluebird." Matt pointed to the back of the campground. "I saw a handicapped sticker in the window. Haven't met them yet. And right after you two left, a couple pulling a little popup travel trailer came in. It's that gray and white one down there on the other side of that big oak. Young couple. They walked by here on their way to the pool. Stopped and talked awhile. Jerry and Trina Hancock. They're here for a couple of days. He had a Blackberry or something like that hooked to his belt. Could have been one of those new GPS units, or a cell phone, though."

"There are so many different electronic things these days...Blackberries and IPhones and Palms and Droids and heaven knows what else is out there now. The only way I find out about them is from the kids at school," Julie said.

"I know," Matt replied. "We have to try and keep up with all that crap in the department. You know, we can't let the bad guys get ahead of us. I hope somebody thinks up an app for that."

"Matt, dear?" Rachel said. "Are the coals ready? I'm really hungry."

"Right to it, hon," Matt replied.

The late afternoon sun had slipped behind a bank of clouds and the temperature had fallen from sweltering to slightly uncomfortable, so they ate outside at the picnic table. The chicken breasts were marinated in teriyaki sauce and grilled to perfection, and the salad was full of all the good stuff – green peppers, celery, onions, mushrooms, tomatoes and cucumbers.

"That was delicious, brother dear. Thanks," Julie sighed.

"You're welcome. We grill out a lot in the summer. Heck, sometimes we make a meal just on a big salad."

"There's no way I could get Mike Alexander to eat *just* a salad. He has to have his red meat, and lots of it. And if I really want to see him inhale his food, I just add gravy. Don't get near his plate. He's like a dog guarding his bowl."

Matt laughed. "Look sis, if you want to lose the weight and keep it off, you have to change your diet. And it has to be a permanent change. Not just until you lose the weight. Eat more salad, fish and turkey or chicken and give Michael his red meat. You'll both be happy."

"I know. I'll have to try it when he gets here."

After supper, Julie helped Rachel wash and dry dishes. Matt decided to scare up some wood for a fire. "And don't tell me it's too hot for a campfire. It's never too hot," he said.

"What a pyro," Rachel laughed and gently smacked his shoulder.

He returned with an armful of limbs and branches and dropped them into the fire pit. He then made a teepee with the small branches, and set the larger limbs aside to add later. "I'm gonna wait for it to get dark before I light this."

"Fine with me," Julie replied.

He eased into the reclining chair and twisted opened a cold beer.

"So how's work?" Julie asked.

"Nothing major going on right now. Must be too hot for the bad guys. I figured it was a good time to do this."

"I know he loves what he does, but he's a workaholic," Rachel said. "Sometimes I think if he doesn't slow down he's gonna crash and burn."

Matt scowled. "Hey, we only have two detectives in our department, Sarah and me. That doesn't leave either of us with a lot of down time. I realize Alton isn't a hot bed of criminal activity, but someone has to be on duty – just in case. The only reason I'm here is that we agreed to take each other's cases when one of us is on vacation or away at a class or something."

Rachel looked at Julie. "A source of contention, as you can see."

"I know what you mean. I think Mike works way too much. But he just had to have his own dealership. Now he wants Chris to come and work for him. I know what he's doing. He thinks Chris will be there to take over when he decides to retire. We've had a few discussions about it, and I told him I think he needs to slow down a little. But if that's what he wants…" she threw her hands up in mock surrender.

"Amen," Rachel said. Matt sat back and quietly sipped his beer. He knew never to try and win an argument with two women. Best just to be seen and not heard.

All three were lounging outside enjoying the early evening when John and Rose Maynard walked across the street from their camper.

"Goin' down to the pavilion tonight?" John asked.

Matt looked up. "What's going on down there?"

"A kid from town's comin' to entertain us. They say he can sing real good. Gonna start about eight thirty or so. Everybody's goin'. How about it?"

"You know. I didn't even look at the events calendar for today. But I'm up for that," Julie replied. "It's going to be a beautiful night. Well guys?"

Matt sat up in his chair. "Sure. We'll put some beer and wine in the cooler and head down. See you there."

Travis Jameson could sing, and his guitar playing was exceptional. The young man from Riverton showed off his talents to the campers by singing some old country favorites – songs sung by Johnny Cash, Conway Twitty, and Willie Nelson to name a few, and he sprinkled in a few newer ones from current entertainers – Garth Brooks, Randy Travis, and Kenny Chesney – for good measure.

The three of them sat on one side of a picnic table. Julie scanned the area. "Looks like a full house."

Rachel smiled. "Yeah, they'd be sorry if they missed this guy. He's good."

Someone had built a large bon fire nearby and a few people brought marshmallows to roast. Travis performed for almost forty five minutes and received a standing ovation after his last song, not to mention a few bucks in his tip jar. After he left, everyone moved over around the fire.

"He's got a real good voice, don't you think?" Lois Yates asked.

Tom Pettyjohn replied, "He's got a great voice. We'd better remember his name. Likely he'll be on the Grand Ole Opry one of these days."

Julie noticed a couple sitting away from the fire. He was smoking a cigarette and staring into the flames; she was sitting in a wheelchair. Julie walked over and introduced herself.

"Hi, I'm Julie Alexander."

"Hello, I'm Ken Atwater. This is my wife, Lydia."

"That was a nice little concert," Julie said.

"Yes, it was," Ken answered. "The young man has a good voice."

"He sure does. How long are you staying here at the campground?"

"Oh, probably a week or so. We're from New Jersey and we're new to camping. We just got the motor home about a month ago, and we're still getting used to it."

"Ken is a golfer," Lydia added.

He arched his bushy eyebrows. "Not a very good one, mind you. Nobody on the PGA Champion's Tour needs to be nervous. But I hack away every chance I get. I promised myself that when I retired that I'd play a game of golf in every state. I found a golf course over in Doniphan. It's called Sycamore Hills Country Club. I think I'll try my luck there tomorrow.

"A game of golf in every state? That's quite a challenge," Julie said.

"What about you?" Ken asked.

"Actually I'm here for the week with my brother and sister-in-law. My husband will be down Friday after work."

"Oh, so you don't work?" Lydia asked.

"Oh yes, we both do. I teach high school geometry and he owns a car dealership."

"Then you really *do* work. I work from home." Her eyes lowered. "I was in an automobile accident ten years ago and injured my back. I'm stuck in this thing now." She tapped the wheels of her chair. "But I still have my brain and I can type pretty well, so I dabble in the stock market and buy things on Ebay," she said.

"The bastard got off with a fine and a lousy six months in jail," Ken growled.

"Ken, please stop!" Lydia frowned. "I'm sorry, Julie. He just can't let it go."

Ken sighed heavily. "A cross I gladly bear." He turned to his wife. "I'm bushed. Ready to go, dear?"

"Yes, I think so." She looked up at Julie. "It was a pleasure to meet you. Maybe we'll see you tomorrow. Good night."

"Good night. Nice to meet you, too. If you need help with anything, I'm on site twelve on Robin's Nest Lane."

"We'll keep that in mind," Ken said. He grabbed the handles of the wheelchair and pushed it back toward their campsite.

Julie heard Stan Yates talking and walked back toward the group.

"The guy's really weird," Stan said.

"What guy are you talking about?" Julie asked.

"Frank Willis. You know, the skinny guy in the beat up old camper."

"What about him?"

Stan continued, "Sonny told me…"

"Who's Sonny?"

Stan rolled his eyes. "The maintenance guy. Anyway, Sonny told me about old Frank. Seems Frank's wife died a few years ago after some kind of botched surgery somewhere in New Jersey. He sued and got a big settlement. He stays in that camper all day playing on his computer and talkin' on that ham radio and only goes out after dark. Maybe he's a vampire, huh?"

"I think it's sad. Sometimes bad things just happen," Lois Yates replied. "We lost our daughter twelve years ago. She was seven."

The group was suddenly quiet.

"She...was abducted and...they found her body a week later." Her eyes welled with tears. "They're still looking for the killer. We...we blamed ourselves for a long time after that, but the psychiatrist said we did everything right. It wasn't our fault. Sometimes bad things just happen."

Stan said, "There's no statute of limitations on murder so we have faith that the police will catch him." He looked over at his wife with loving eyes, and she took his hand. "You ready to go, sweetheart?" he asked softly. She nodded. "Have a good evening everyone," Stan said. He put his arm around her shoulder and they walked away.

Rachel sensed the mood around the fire had darkened considerably. She turned to Jerry and Trina. "How about you guys? How long do you plan to stay?"

"Only a couple of days," Jerry replied.

"We're on a treasure hunt," Trina added. "Have you ever heard of geo treasure hunting?"

"No. What is it?"

"It's on the Internet. You go on their website, geotreasures.com, and they give you a bunch of numbers. Coordinates that relate to a geographic location. You put them in your GPS unit to find the location. Then you go there and find a clue."

"What kind of clue?" Rachel asked.

"Oh, usually it's a five to ten digit number. Occasionally it's a word. You go back to the website, enter the clue and get another set of coordinates. This can go on sometimes for weeks.

Eventually you get a coordinate that has a final clue. If you're the first to enter the final clue on the web site, you're the grand prize winner."

"And what might that be?"

"Anything from gift certificates to vacation trips to money. This time it's ten thousand dollars."

"Ten thousand bucks! For entering clues on a web site? Where do I sign up?" Julie said.

Jerry glared at Trina. "It's not just entering numbers on a web site. You have to travel around and find the location. It's not easy. And we're not sure if it's that much."

"Geo treasure hunting, ya say?" Tom Pettyjohn asked.

"Yes," Jerry replied.

"I've heard of something like that. Some folks call it geocaching. Sounds pretty interesting."

Jerry sensed a moment where he could show off his knowledge on the subject. "Geocaching is different. With geocaching you get only one coordinate, and you use your GPS to find it. One coordinate – one prize. And most times, if you take the prize, you have to replace it with something of equal value. That way everybody who goes to that coordinate will find something. It's basically just for fun. But geo treasure hunting, that's for people who want more than just a little plastic toy or a coupon for a five dollar sub sandwich. They do it for the adventure. It's like geocaching on steroids. Lots of coordinates and clues but only one big prize. And it's finders keepers – losers weepers."

"So, if I was to try one, I might want to do the geocaching first," Tom said.

"Yeah, that would be the best thing. Then you'll learn the basics before jumping into the hard core world of geo treasure hunting."

Tom nodded. "I think I remember somethin' in the newspaper a while back about a searcher dying during one of those treasure hunts. Am I right?"

"Yeah...I remember that, too. Trina and I were just starting to play the treasure hunt games when that happened. I think he was an older guy. Something about slipping and falling off a ledge. It was pretty bad."

"They put clues in dangerous places like that?" Tom asked.

"Well, not normally. I really don't know much about how he died. It really is a safe sport."

Matt was bored but tried to keep up the conversation. "Sounds like fun."

"It is, and you get to see a lot of the country." Jerry turned to his wife. "Well, babe, you ready to go? Gotta be up early."

Trina nodded sheepishly. Jerry grabbed her arm firmly and guided her away from the group.

"Ten thousand dollars," Julie whispered. "That's what I call a real treasure hunt."

Matt looked over at Julie and Rachel and said, "Hey, dynamic duo. The day has finally caught up with me. Are you two ready to go?"

"Sure hon. Goodnight everyone," Rachel said.

They strolled back to their campsites enjoying the gentle breeze and distant chorus of tree frogs and crickets. "Nice group of people. So sad about Stan and Lois losing their daughter," Rachel said.

"Yeah, that's just awful," Julie replied. "And what about the big money duo? We should check out that website. What was it? Geotreasures.com? Did you bring your laptop?"

"As a matter of fact I did. Let's do it tomorrow sometime."

"Maybe we can win the big bucks," Julie said.

"Hah!"

They stood outside by the front door of Julie's bus. She yawned and stretched her aching muscles. "Well you two, I'm outta here. Another round of ibuprofen and I should sleep well tonight. What time are we hiking?"

"How about after breakfast? Beat the heat," Rachel said.

"Sounds good. See you tomorrow."

Chapter 10

December, 1864
Oregon County Missouri

Skunk finished his coffee and leaned closer to the fire; a thin trail of smoke twisted and danced in the frigid air. He pulled the wool blanket over his shoulders and shivered. *Damn cold. Can't wait to git home.*

His real name was William, but he came by his nickname rightly, as anyone who stood too close to him could confirm. He never took a bath; the only time he got wet was when it rained or he sloshed through a stream. His tattered shirt and pants hadn't seen a bar of soap since the day he donned them. But cleanliness wasn't high on Skunk's list of priorities - killing and getting back home were.

He picked up his rifle and began to polish the long barrel with his grimy sleeve. "Well, Lucy, ole girl, we're gittin' perty good at this. Easy as pickin' off squirrels on a branch, right? Hell, we don't need ta belong ta no army ta kill Yanks. Besides, we ain't the only ones what left when the fightin' started. Lots of 'em took off fer high ground. General Lee ain't missin' us now anyways."

He slowly rubbed his calloused hand over the worn stock and grinned. "Let's see now. I'm countin' pert near...hell, there's so many notches in your butt I cain't count 'em all, girl." Truth was Skunk had never learned to count. Never even went to school.

The only thing he learned to do well was shoot his rifle. "I know folks back home, they's gonna be so proud of what we done."

Skunk turned to the other rifle lying on the ground next to him. "How 'bout you? You wanna take some Yanks out, too. That's funny, ain't it Lucy. A Yank gun killin' Yanks." He laughed and glanced over at the pile of dead animals. "Lucy, we're gonna find somebody ta buy them there critters. They's gonna make us enough money ta get ta Vicksburg. Cain't wait ta git home."

"Damn, girl. It's cold!" He laid the rifle on the ground next to him and rolled out two more blankets. Then he put the coffee pot on the ground next to the fire, sat back against a small tree and lit a cigarette.

Suddenly, he heard branches breaking behind him. He leaped up and whirled around. Victoria was standing five feet away, her skinning knife pointed at his face.

"Whoa now, little lady! What's this all about?"

Victoria glared at Skunk. "You. You're a murderer. You killed my papa. Those animals are from his traps. You shot him dead. And you'll pay for that."

"What you talkin about, girl? Why...I trapped these here critters myself."

She stood defiantly. "Then where are your traps?"

"Uh...I...I got 'em all round here everwhere."

"Round here, you say?" Victoria said sarcastically.

"Sure 'nuf."

"This is my papa's land. You came here and you killed him and took his skins." Then she saw the rifle lying on the ground near the fire. "That's his gun! You took it when you murdered him."

Skunk squinted in the dim light and looked closely at Victoria. "Say, don't I know you? Ain't you the little lady what gave me that stew yesterday?"

"I should have let you starve."

Skunk smiled and looked at the knife in her hand. "Darlin,' you honestly think you can take me with that there little pig sticker?"

She glanced at her hip. *The gun...too late.* Besides, she felt more comfortable with the knife. "I've skinned bigger animals than you with this. Now, do as I say. Give me that rope."

"I kinda like a woman with spunk. And I was right, you are rather fetchin'."

Her knuckles turned white as she gripped the knife tighter. "Maybe I won't kill you. Maybe I'll just cut you. It would only be a small cut, but one that will take away your legs. Then maybe I'll let you die out here, like you let my papa die." Victoria suddenly stopped. *No, Papa wouldn't want me to do that.* "Now, I said give me that rope."

He stooped down and touched a rabbit carcass. "Ya mean this 'un here?"

"Do it. Now!" Victoria shouted.

Skunk removed the rope from the dead rabbit. Suddenly, he reached up and slapped the knife out of her hand; it flew into the nearby tall grass. He grabbed for her. She screamed and quickly backed out of his reach. He lunged at her, but she drew the gun from its holster and swerved from his grasp. She stepped back again, tripped on the pile of dead animals, and fell to the ground. The gun went off; its bullet struck Skunk in the left shoulder and sunk into soft flesh. He spun and fell, blood oozing from the wound. "Ya shot me, ya little injun. I'll gitcha fer that!"

Victoria scrambled to her feet and raced into the nearby tall grass.

"I'll gitcha, ya little Yank injun. You cain't outrun me."
Skunk clutched his shoulder. "I kilt yer pa, did I? Well, how
'bout I just kill you, too. One good arm's all I need ta wring yer
perty little neck!"

She could hear his footsteps close behind. The tall grass
slapped at her face, pulling, grabbing at her, holding her back.
She couldn't see, so she dropped the heavy gun at her feet,
shielded her eyes with both hands and pushed forward. Her
breath came hard; her heart raced in her chest. She blindly
veered off to her left and suddenly found herself in an open field,
with only two small maple trees, their limbs drooping and bare to
greet her. A large hollowed-out oak tree lay at the far end of the
field a hundred feet away. A hundred feet...to Victoria it may as
well have been a hundred miles.

Her feet felt as if they were frozen to the hard ground.
"Mama!" she screamed in terror.

Just then she thought she heard someone whisper. "Victoria."

She spun to her left and saw the silhouette of a woman
standing in the twilight, her arms open, beaconing her to come
closer. Victoria squinted at the dimly lit figure.

"Victoria, come here."

"Mama?"

Chapter 11

Big Forest Campground
Riverton, Missouri

Frank stumbled into his trailer. *Jesus, that was close*! He slammed the door and leaned against it, gasping for air. Sweat burned his eyes and he lunged toward the breakfast booth. He swung his body onto the slick, tattered vinyl seat. His eyes were wide with fright. *Get a grip. They didn't recognize me. I know they didn't.*

Frank Willis had just crossed paths with his worst nightmare – Ken and Lydia Atwater. Seeing them brought back a flood of memories - the accident...the crushed car...Lydia trapped in the front seat and soaked in her own blood...the cops...the judge...the jail.

After he'd served his six months, he wanted to move away, but then Stella got sick. *Why did we stay? Why did she have to die?* He couldn't go outside anymore, not in the daylight. That's when people pointed at him and whispered. "Look! There's the idiot who was trying to make a call on his cell phone, crossed the center line and hit that poor woman." Without his beloved Stella the whispers turned to screams. He moved away, far away, and changed his name. *Oh, Stella, honey. I miss you so much.*

This is crazy! He took several deep breaths. *Relax. Calm down. They didn't see me. And so what if they did? What can they do to me now? Nothing! Now is not the time to wig out, Frankie boy. You've got things to do.*

The fear finally subsided, and he reached for his laptop. He took another deep breath. *It's night time. The right time. Time to play.*

He loved the night; its blackness held that special power. And Frank needed the power. It kept him one step ahead of his enemies, the ones who wanted all that he had. Nothing else mattered anymore, not food or showers or conversations with intellectuals - just winning. He had lost at life, he had lost his Stella. But he was winning at this game, the geo treasure hunt game.

He snickered at the thought of winning another prize. *Those techie nerds. They think they can change the way the earth revolves with their GPS' and 3G wireless notebooks. What do they know!* Frank knew the secret – the night!

The geotreasures.com website always had several treasure hunts going at one time in various parts of the country. That way everybody had a chance to pick up a prize without burning up a lot of gas. Frank focused on those hunts close to home – that being southern Missouri and northern Arkansas. During a treasure hunt, the website always posted the coordinates between midnight and three a.m. each Tuesday morning. Most normal people were sleeping at that time. But Willis, who slept during the day and roamed at night, could easily record the coordinates and enter them into his GPS unit. Then he would sneak out into the darkness and find the hidden treasure before anyone else could get there. Oh, every so often someone would beat him to it, but he was always high on the list of repeat winners. He had mastered the game, and he loved it.

Shortly after midnight he was finally ready to play. "Well, let's get this show on the road," he said to himself.

He accessed the website and registered as returning player ITISMINE. He located the coordinates and entered them into his

GPS. Then from the main menu, he clicked on the bar titled *Chat Room*. It was used by searchers to talk about the current treasure hunt. Frank used it to tease those who thought they might be closing in on the prize. One of the players he regularly taunted was *FINDEM*, a treasurer hunter who had come in second to ITISMINE on several previous hunts. Tonight would be no different. Frank knew he would get to the location first, and wanted to dig FINDEM one last time.

His thin fingers clicked on the keys. *Hey FINDEM. U out there? Just want u 2 know I'll be thinking of u as I drink a beer on a beach in Mexico after I get the 10 grand. You're just 2 slow, buddy. Tell u what, I'll wear a blindfold on the next quest. Maybe you'll get lucky. LOL. Don't bother showing up for this one because…ITISMINE!*

He smirked. "That ought to piss him off."

He signed off the website and shut down the computer. *Let's do it, Stella. Let's go get the goodies.* He walked to the fridge and pulled out another beer, picked up a flashlight from the broken-down recliner leaning near the front door and stepped out into the blessed night. At the back of his camper he grabbed a small, rusty shovel, slung it over his shoulder and walked quietly toward the office at the front of the campground. He stopped along the way to pee near a large oak tree. *Damn beer. Does it to me every time.*

He followed the GPS coordinates of the final clue; it was safely hidden under a pile of large rocks next to the light pole by the campground office. And as far as Frank figured, he was the closest searcher. At the rock pile he scanned the area to make sure no one was watching. Confident he was alone he put down his beer and began to remove the rocks.

Ten minutes later he had enough rock cleared away to start digging. "Makin' me work for this one," he puffed. He took a big swig of beer; he was thirsty. The ground was soft, and the shovel sank in with ease. Twenty minutes later Frank had a large pit about three feet wide and two feet deep.

How deep did they stash this thing anyway? He stomped on the shovel again; this time the blade hit something hard. *Finally!* He knelt down and brushed off the remaining dirt to reveal a small metal container about the size of a cigar box. He grabbed the box and climbed out of the hole, sat down in the freshly dug dirt and wiped the sweat from his brow with the back of his hand. He flipped open the lid and saw a folded piece of gold colored paper.

"Well, hello there. Come to Papa." He picked the paper out of the box and unfolded it to see a final series of numbers. He chuckled softly, "I love it!"

He finished his beer and tossed the can and the empty box back into the hole. *This is so cool.* He filled the hole and covered it with the rocks. "Maybe I'll come back and watch 'em dig. That would be fun." He raised his arms in victory and did a small dance around the hole. "Once again, ITISMINE wins."

Frank looked at his watch. It was one twenty five in the morning and he was the winner again. *Now, off to the camper. Ten grand here I come.* Just as he turned toward the campground, he noticed a figure dressed in long sweatpants and a hooded sweatshirt standing by the office. *What a yutz. Sweats. In this heat. I'm outta here.* Frank shoved the gold paper in his pants pocket and walked to the parking lot. He thought he heard footsteps behind him. *Is that idiot following me? Enough of this crap.*

He turned and faced the hooded figure. "Who the hell are you?"

"Why, ITISMINE. It's me, FINDEM. I thought you would be here."

Frank squinted. "You're...FINDEM?"

"That I am."

"Well FINDEM, I'm sorry to say you're too late again," Frank chuckled. He pulled the gold paper from his pocket and tauntingly waved it in the air.

FINDEM spoke softly. "I see you've recovered from your injuries."

Frank cocked his head. His heart began to thump loudly in his chest. "How...how do you know about my injuries?"

"Why ITISMINE, I was there the night you picked up a clue for one of our hunts. It was at a rest stop near Memphis, wasn't it? Last summer, if I recall correctly."

Frank's knees began to shake. "Yeah...it was."

"What do you remember about that night?" FINDEM asked.

"Not much. Why?" Frank's mouth was getting dry. He wished he hadn't finished off that beer.

"Oh, I'm just curious. Come on, tell me what you remember."

"I...I remember parking my car and walking to the trash can and finding the envelope. After that...I woke up in the hospital. They told me it was a hit and run driver and that I fell into a big ditch."

"That's all? Shame on you. Not a very good memory. Well, why don't you let me fill in the gaps? You're right, it was a hit and run driver. But it was more like you were thrown into the ravine next to the off ramp. It was a very deep ravine, ITISMINE."

"I...I thought I was the only one there."

"So wrong you are again. And that awful person who hit you...shame on them, too. They left you for dead. But, I see you recovered. I'm really sorry I couldn't stop to help you. Other cars were pulling into the rest stop."

Frank stared at the shadow standing in front of him. Sweat drizzled down his face; his breath came in short spurts now. "It was you? You tried to kill me? For a lousy prize?"

"It's not about the lousy prize, ITISMINE. No, it's about you winning all the *lousy* prizes *all* the time," FINDEM seethed.

"But I don't win all the time. Other people get prizes. Not just me!"

"Oh, yes. I do seem to remember another player who won quite often. He was out there playing the search game before you joined up. Sad about him, though. It seems he died during a hunt in Cleveland. Fell off a cliff, I think. Do you remember?"

Frank's eyes were wide with fright. "No, I...I don't."

"You see, ITISMINE, you shouldn't always win. Everyone needs a chance to share in these prizes. Don't you think?" FINDEM whispered.

Frank nodded, his tongue stuck to the roof of his mouth.

FINDEM moved closer. "So, how about I win this one, hmm?"

Frank shoved the paper back into his pocket. "You're not serious."

"You're a bright boy, ITISMINE. You figure it out."

Julie stepped inside the bus and turned on the TV to watch what was left of the late news. Around ten thirty she changed into her sleep shirt and went to bed. Sometime during the night, a hot flash disrupted her sleep; she woke briefly and stuck her foot out from under the sheet. *That's better.* Half an hour later a second hot flash hit. This time she woke to find herself sweating. She flipped the sheet off and lay still in the bed, hoping the hot flashes would diminish. A few minutes later she was sweating again.

She launched herself out of bed and stomped down the hall toward the thermostat. *I hate this. When are they going to stop?* She dialed the thermostat back a few degrees and sat in the recliner while the cool air wafted over her. *Finally! Better now. Let's try this again.*

On her way to the bedroom, she stopped to look out the window at the now sleeping campground. Several street lights placed strategically around the area softly illuminated two or three campers, leaving the rest in darkness.

Then she saw it, a shadowy figure skulking behind the office.

"That's odd," she wondered aloud. "It's still warm outside. Why would someone be wearing a sweatshirt?"

The figure was running toward the area of the hiking trails, carrying something. It looked like some kind of rolled up towel. She squinted. *Am I dreaming? Who in the world is that? And what are they doing out in the middle of the night? They're going the wrong way for a midnight swim.*

The figure stopped briefly in the playground area near the swing set, crouched to the ground, scanned the area, then stood and ran toward the trailhead. Julie watched. *I'm not dreaming!* She was wide awake now, and decided to wait and watch a little longer. *Maybe they'll come back.* The clock over the stove read one fifty-five.

Several minutes passed. Then she saw the mysterious figure again. But something was different now. The rolled up towel was gone. *This is just too weird.* The figure jogged toward the far end of the campground and disappeared into the darkness. Julie waited by the window for another five minutes, but all was dark and still. The mysterious midnight jogger was gone. *Well, that certainly was interesting. I'll have to ask around tomorrow.*

See if anyone else saw that.   She climbed back into bed and eventually drifted off to sleep.

The alarm jolted Sonny Wallace awake at five thirty. The sun was breaking the horizon; the morning sky blushed a pale crimson. He pulled himself out of his recliner ran to his bedroom and changed into his dark blue maintenance shirt and pants and ran his fingers through his hair to straighten out last night's muss. After a breakfast of toast and coffee, he stepped out of the camper, reluctantly ready to start his long day.

He hired on at the park last July when he answered a want ad in the Oregon County Globe. A loner, Sonny traveled the country picking up odd jobs to keep him in cigarettes and beer. One of the perks of this job was free room and board. The park always had one or two older camping units available to rent out, and Sonny lucked into one. Not having to pay rent meant he could buy more beer.

He ran through the day's work list in his head. *First thing this morning I gotta clean the pool and check the chlorine levels. Can't have any nasty germs in there with the little kiddies. And there's another light out over at the deep end. Want to get that done before anybody shows up. Next, gotta clean the bath house, then mow the grass and trim around the equipment shed. Hell, today's gonna be a bitch. If I get that pool done before eight, I'll be damned lucky. And it feels like it's gonna be another hot one.*

He smelled the aroma of fresh brewed coffee coming from the office. *Damn, she's already up. Better get with it. Don't want my pay docked again.* He rounded the corner of the work shed, and almost stepped in a large spot of a dark liquid on the concrete walk.

"What the hell?" He knelt down and looked closely at the substance.

"Blood? Huh. Coyote musta got a rabbit." His eyes followed the blood trail toward the pool entrance. "Damn. That's all I need is to have to scrub the pool out." He stood and walked to the pool gate, which was standing wide open. He paused and squinted into the darkened pool area. "Somethin' ain't right."

He rushed to the pool's edge. Suddenly he saw it. Floating face down in the shallow end was a frail looking body; the surrounding water swirled bright red. He recognized the floating corpse and jumped into the knee deep water. "Donna! Hey Donna! Come quick! It's Frank!"

Chapter 12

Big Forest Campground

"Julie! Julie, come on. Wake up!" Rachel banged on the camper door. The noise roused Julie from a deep sleep.

"Okay, okay, I'm up. Coming." She scrambled down the hall, and opened the door to a wide-eyed Rachel.

"Julie, get dressed. There's a dead body in the pool."

"What?"

"Yeah, the maintenance guy found it this morning. Matt's down there right now."

"Oh my God, who is it? What happened?"

"I don't know. Right after he heard the sirens, he got a call and left in a hurry. Come on, let's go see."

Julie rushed back to the bedroom and put on yesterday's shorts, tee shirt and shoes. Heading toward the pool area, the two women saw Carolyn Pettyjohn standing at the edge of the road. "What's going on? Is it a fire?" Carolyn asked.

"We're not sure, Carolyn," Rachel replied. "We'll let you know."

The office and pool were located about two hundred yards from the main campground. Julie and Rachel saw two Alton police cruisers, an ambulance and a fire truck clogging the entrance. Matt was standing in the driveway holding his digital camera and talking with one of the patrolmen while the other officer cordoned off the parking lot and the pool area with yellow crime scene tape.

Sonny stood nearby smoking a cigarette; his hands shook noticeably.   Stan Yates was leaning on the hood of the ambulance and acknowledged the women with a nod.

"What's going on, Stan?" Rachel asked.

"Don't know yet. That's your hubby over there, isn't it?"

"Yes, he's a detective with the Alton police department."

"Lucky him."

Rachel pouted. "Depends on how you look at it. I have a feeling he's not on vacation anymore."

The three watched Matt walk over to Donna. They were too far away to hear the conversation, but saw Matt jot notes on a small pad of paper. Donna was very animated, waving her hands and pointing back toward Frank's camper. Matt nodded and said something to her and she smiled weakly and walked to the office door where Phil and Eric stood.

Matt turned and walked toward the three onlookers.

"We won't interfere, Matt. What happened?" Rachel asked.

"Sonny over there found Frank Willis floating in the pool, but Frank didn't need a life vest."

"Frank Willis?"

"Yeah, the guy in the ratty old camper up there. Donna called 911 and all hell broke loose. After I got the call from the station, I grabbed the camera and ran down here to take some preliminary pictures for the crime scene techs." Matt knew the medical examiner would want to see how the body looked when it was first discovered, and there was no better way than with digital photos. Thank goodness for those little memory cards that can hold hundreds of pictures.

He looked toward Stan and asked, "Were you here when Sonny found Frank?"

Stan shook his head. "Nope. I was still asleep. Sonny's yellin' woke me. Anything you need from me?"

"Yes. We'll need to talk to you and Lois along with everyone else in the park. Why don't you go back to your camper? Someone from the police department will be by later."

"We'll be waitin' for ya," Stan said and slowly walked toward Robin's Nest Lane.

Matt turned to the women. "This is a first for me. We just don't have a lot of dead bodies down here so I called the county for help in processing the scene. They're sending Sean and a couple of other techs. And Sarah just got here, too. She's gonna help with interviews. I sent one of the uniforms over to Willis' trailer to tape it off. Once the techs get here, they'll do their magic and then get the body to the M.E. for autopsy. We'll know more then."

He surveyed the scene again. "I'm pretty sure foul play is involved here. There's a large amount of blood in one spot and the trail runs from the parking lot all the way over to the pool. Maybe Frank was trying to get to the office for help. I don't know. As soon as I'm done here, I'll head over to process Willis' trailer. After that I'll start interviewing people."

Julie's mind snapped back to the mysterious night runner. "Matt, I saw something last night. It was really weird. I got up about one thirty or so and saw someone running toward the trailhead."

"What were you doing up at one thirty in the morning?"

"My own private summer, if you must know."

"Oh…running, huh? Could you tell who it was?"

"No, it was too dark. But it looked like they had a hooded sweatshirt or something."

"Toward the trailhead?"

"Yeah. And I think they were carrying something, maybe a rolled up towel."

"Anything else?"

"About ten minutes later they came running back toward the campground, but they didn't have the rolled up thing anymore."

Matt jotted the information in his note book. "I'll send somebody over that way and see if they can find anything. If you remember any more, let me know."

"I will."

"There's not much more to see here. I told Donna I'll be interviewing everyone in the campground and to not let anyone leave before I talk to them. I hope to have the autopsy results later this afternoon or this evening. I think the crime scene is the parking lot where the largest pool of blood is. And it looks like Willis staggered to the edge of the pool and fell in. We'll check his trailer and the rest of the campground just in case. When I'm done with interviews, I'll have to go back to the station. Looks like my vacation is over – at least for now."

Rachel sighed and nodded. "I know."

"Then you two might as well go back and try to make the best of it 'til this thing is finished. I'll stop by before I go to town."

"Do you think we can go on our hike?" Julie asked.

"I don't think that's such a good idea, sis. There may still be a killer out there. I'd feel better if you two stayed close to the campsite today."

"Okay, we'll just walk in the campground."

Both women, still shaken by the morning's events, walked slowly back to their campsites.

"This is like a nightmare. Who would do this?" Julie asked.

Rachel shook her head. "I don't know. Maybe he was on a late night walk and got mugged. Or maybe he came across somebody trying to break into the office."

"Man, what a way to die."

"I know."

Julie said, "And what about the guy I saw running through here last night. You don't think it could be someone in the campground, do you?"

They stopped and looked at each other. "You're making the hair on the back of my neck stand up," Rachel said. "I guess it's possible, but I sure hope not."

Rounding the corner onto Robin's Nest, they saw John and Rose Maynard talking with Lois Yates.

"What happened?" John asked.

"The maintenance man found a body in the pool," Rachel said.

"Who was it?"

"Frank Willis, the guy in the old camper."

"Is he dead?" Lois asked.

"Yes, but we don't know any more than that."

"Oh my word, how horrible," Rose added.

"Yes, my husband, Matt, is a police detective. He has been called in to work on this case."

"But we didn't see or hear anything," Lois said.

John piped up. "No, we didn't either."

"Well, I'm sure the police will want to talk to each of us, so just be sure you tell detective Baker everything you can remember," Rachel said using Matt's official title.

They walked on silently, their thoughts about Frank Willis' violent death. When they arrived at the campsite, Julie asked. "Well, now what?"

"I don't know about you, but I need to eat something, comb my hair and brush my teeth," Rachel replied.

"Sounds like a plan. Want to come over to my place? I'll make some coffee and I have cranberry juice. I want to call Mike, too."

"Okay, let me get my yogurt and I'll be right over."

Julie went into the bus and called home. "Everything is fine, Mike. Matt is lead detective on the case, and Rachel and I are staying close to the campers."

"Are you sure?" Mike asked, his voice indicating some concern for her safety.

"Yes, dear, don't worry. I'll call you if anything changes. See you Friday."

"I should be there with you, Julie."

"Mike, it's okay. Really. Rachel's here. I'll be fine. I love you, honey."

"I love you too, Julie. Call me if you need me."

"I will."

The two women ate breakfast inside, then took their coffee outside and sat at the picnic table.

"Is there a killer among us, Rachel?" Julie asked.

"I don't know. Jeez, I hope not. That's a scary thought. I can't believe any of these people could do it. But we've only known them for a few hours. We have no idea what they're capable of."

Julie added. "And we know zippo about Frank Willis."

Rachel sipped her coffee. "Well, we *do* know that he came into a lot of money after his wife died, right?"

Julie nodded.

"And we know he had a computer and went out after dark."

"Yeah, so, what does that mean?"

"I don't have a freakin' clue. Heck, maybe he carried a lot of cash on him and someone killed him for it. Who knows?"

Julie looked up. "I think I might stroll over to the trailhead later and see if I can find anything."

Rachel stared at her sister-in-law. "Are you nuts? You heard what Matt said. The killer could still be out there."

"But I know I saw something."

"So let the police do their job and find it."

"But what if they don't?"

"Then there was nothing out there to find!"

"I didn't dream it, Rachel."

"I didn't say you did, Julie. I'm just saying it could be dangerous and you need to let Matt take care of it."

"Okay, okay. You're right. I'll stay out of their way. I just can't help it. That was just so weird seeing that guy running and carrying...whatever it was."

Chapter 13

December, 1864
Oregon County Missouri

The rifle blast split the morning calm and startled Victoria awake. She lay still for a moment, trying to get her bearings. Suddenly she remembered. *Uncle. The killer.* She scrambled out of the hollowed-out tree trunk and rushed across the open field toward the sound. The tall, unforgiving grass again tried to hold her back, but she flailed through it with abandon. She eventually stumbled back into the camp site and found Francois standing guard over Skunk. Breathless, she rushed toward her uncle.

"Are you alright?" he asked.

"Yes, I let him get too close and he knocked my knife out of my hand."

Francois was holding the pistol Victoria had dropped. "I found him with this. How did he get it?" he asked.

"I know. I dropped it when I ran into the grass. I'm sorry."

Skunk looked up at Francois. "See, I told ya I ain't kilt her." He turned to Victoria, "Where'd you go, young'un? I was right behind ya, and then you was just gone."

"My mama…" she hesitated. Better he didn't know about that. "Oh, you're such a stupid man." She raised her head in defiance. "I am Cherokee. I can make myself into a tree or a rock or an eagle and you'll never find me."

Francois returned the gun and knife to Victoria. He then raised his rifle. "Victoria, are we ready to do this?"

"Yes, Uncle."

Francois glared at Skunk. "Mister, what is your name?"

"The name's Skunk Adams. What's it to you?"

"It matters nothing to me. But you killed my brother and this child's papa. You then steal his pelts and his gun. You will die for that."

Skunk's mind raced to save his life. "I tell ya, I ain't kilt nobody."

"You lie!" Victoria screamed. "Why did you do it?"

Skunk grimaced from the pain in his shoulder. He took a deep breath. "You really wanna know? I'll tell ya like it is. I figerred he was a Yank, and where I'm from the only good Yank is a dead one. This is Confederate dirt y'all are standin' on! There ain't no room here for a Yankee. Me and Lucy, we plugged him when he weren't lookin. Hell, it was easy. One shot, one dead Yank. And it felt good…real good. Another notch in Lucy's butt.   Them pelts, they was gonna pay our way back to Vicksburg. There, I said it. Y'all happy now?"

Victoria screamed. "Murderer!" She drew her skinning knife and rushed toward Skunk. Francois grabbed her by the arm and held her back. "Victoria, let me do it. Stand him up so I can get a good shot."

"Not so fast!" a voice called from the edge of the clearing. Francois and Victoria turned to see Union army soldiers on horseback approaching. "Sir, don't dispatch that man. That's an order," called out one of the soldiers.

"Why not? He killed my brother. He must die for it," Francois yelled back.

"That may be so. But then, sir, I would have to arrest you for murder. Now lower your rifle."

Francois turned to Skunk. "You got lucky today. But one way or another, you will pay for this."

Skunk breathed a deep sigh and looked up at the soldier. "They injunned up on me real quiet like, come up behind me and was gonna kill me. Hell, the young'un, she done shot me once."

The soldier dismounted his horse and walked toward them, his stride clearly spoke of authority. He appeared to be in his early thirties, tall and lean, a bushy, dark brown mustache smothered his mouth. It reminded Victoria of her papa's.

"I am Sergeant Phinneas Smith of the 3rd Missouri State Militia Regiment. What is the fuss here?" he asked Francois.

"This man, he came on to my brother's land, shot and killed him, then stole his pelts and his gun. Me and her, we tracked him and we were going to shoot him."

Sergeant Smith stroked his mustache, pondering Francois' story. "May I inquire as to your brother's name?"

"Henri Levalier, Sergeant. I am Francois Levalier, and she is his daughter. She is an orphan now."

Victoria stood next to her uncle, tears filled her eyes.

"Well Francois Levalier, we will let our court determine whether this man killed your brother." He turned to Skunk. "Sir, what is your name?"

"Abraham Davis. And I ain't kilt nobody."

"Liar!" Victoria yelled. "He says his name is Skunk Adams and he told us killed my papa because he was a Yankee. He said he wanted to go to Vicksburg."

Sergeant Smith's eyes narrowed and he cocked his head. "Vicksburg? Why Vicksburg? If I'm not mistaken I believe we have a Confederate sympathizer here. Or perhaps even a deserter. Am I correct in my assumption, Mr. Adams?"

"I don't need no army to help me kill Yanks. I just want to get outa here, that's all," Skunk replied.

"Well, Mr. Adams, that's not going to happen today. We'll tend to your wound and then you and your accusers will be coming with us." The sergeant turned toward a soldier nearby. "Private Little, bring your bag and patch this man's wound."

The private dropped down off of his horse, collected his medicine bag and proceeded to dress Skunk's shoulder.

Sergeant Smith raised his head and called, "Corporal Wilson, at present I believe we have an outstanding warrant for a bushwhacker named William Adams. Do we not?"

Corporal Wilson was sitting on his horse about fifty feet away from Sergeant Smith. He reached back into his saddle bag and pulled out a stack of papers. He rifled through them, pulled one out, and waved it in the air. "Why, yes we do, Sergeant. Goes by the name Skunk. Says here Skunk Adams is wanted as a bushwhacker and a murderer. They say he killed four people sympathetic to the Union a while back. Might this be him, sir?"

Sergeant Smith smiled wryly. "Why, yes. Yes, I believe it does smell like him. He looked at private Little who was just finishing up his patch job on Skunk's wound. "When you're done, shackle Mr. Adams. He is now our prisoner. And take these rifles."

Smith turned to Francois and Victoria and said. "We've been looking for this man. We will remove him to Fort Davidson where he will be tried. If you accompany us to the fort and testify, it may help to convict him."

Francois looked at Victoria; she nodded. "*Oui*, we will go with you. But the one rifle...it is my brother's. I would like it back."

"Very well, Mr. Levalier. You may have it. We need Mr. Adams' rifle as evidence. It appears by the marks on the stock that he has been a very busy man."

Sergeant Smith gave the order. "Corporal Wilson, let the young lady ride with you."

"Yes, Sergeant." Wilson urged his horse toward Victoria, scooped her up and placed her behind him.

"Mr. Levalier, you may ride with me, sir. Mr. Adams, you will walk. There is no room on a Union horse for a rebel bushwhacker, especially one who stinks to high heaven. Fall in line and move out!" Smith called.

The group began their journey to Fort Davidson. Corporal Wilson turned to Victoria. "What is your name, little lady?"

"My Cherokee name is Eagle Eyes. My English name is Victoria." She gripped his belt tightly.

"It's a pleasure, Miss Victoria. My name is Thomas Wilson." Have you ever been on a horse?" he asked.

"Yes, we have two back at our cabin," she replied. "Their names are Chief and Bear."

"I'm curious. How do you say horse in your native language?"

Victoria thought for a few moments. "You mean Cherokee?"

"Yes, in Cherokee."

"In Cherokee a horse is a *so-qui-li*."

"Well, Gus here, he's a good ole *so-qui-li*, and real gentle. Once you get used to his walk, you'll be fine."

She glanced at the other soldiers. "Why do you wear such strange clothes?"

"We call them uniforms. I'm a corporal in the army, the Union Army."

"What is a corporal?"

"It's a rank and not a very high one at that. It's kind of like being a brave instead of a chief."

"What is the Union Army?"

"Well, a lot of folks get together to fight other folks. You say you're Cherokee?"

"Yes."

"Well, it would be like a bunch of Cherokee Indians gettin' together to fight a bunch of Sioux." Victoria looked puzzled.

"Sioux are Indians, too," he said.

"Oh. But who do you fight?"

"We fight the Confederate Army."

"Why?"

"Because they want to have their own country. You see, our president, President Abraham Lincoln – he's our chief. Well, he doesn't want to have two countries. He wants to keep the country together. And the Union Army wants that, too."

It was very confusing to her, so she opted to talk about something she knew. "But why did that man kill my papa?"

"Well, as for that I can't say, but maybe he thought your papa was on our side, and ole Skunk there is on the Confederate side. We call his kind guerillas and bushwhackers."

"What will happen to him?"

"Well, the last bushwhacker that was tried and found guilty of killing someone, they were sentenced to be shot. My guess is that's what will happen to Mr. Skunk there. We'll remove him from Fort Davidson to Gratiot Prison, up by St. Louis. That's where we take prisoners. Yep, and once he's there, they'll take him out back and shoot him."

"When do we get to the fort?"

"We should arrive in nearly three days."

"Can we hurry?"

"We will surely try, Miss Victoria," he said with a grin. "We will surely try."

Victoria looked around her at a sea of blue uniforms.

"How many others are here with you?"

"Oh, I would say near fifty soldiers, give or take a few."

"That is quite a lot."

"Yes, it is. But we must travel in a large group so we can protect each other from scoundrels like ole' Skunk, there."

Gus' gate was slow and easy, and she soon loosened her grip and relived the events of the previous night. *Did I really see Mama? How could that be? How could she have been there? But, I felt her hug me. At least I think I felt her. We talked to each other. I can't tell Uncle, he'll think I'm ill in the head. I'm glad I'm here and we found Papa's killer.* She chuckled.

"Did you say somethin' missy?" Wilson asked.

"No, but I think that my papa would be pleased with me."

"Why's that?"

"I wasn't afraid and I tracked his killer. My parents named me Eagle Eyes and I'm a great tracker."

"Ya know, it took a lot of melt to do what you did, standin' up to Skunk like that. And shootin' him to boot." He grinned. "Yes, Miss Victoria, I do believe you have given your papa great satisfaction today."

Victoria sat back and swayed to the rhythm of Gus' long, loping gate. "Corporal?"

"Yes, Miss Victoria."

"What's a fort?"

"Why, Miss Victoria, have you never been away from your home?"

"Only to the forest with my papa. He took me to hunt and trap."

Wilson twisted in his saddle and looked back at her. "Well, let me tell you about our fort. It has six walls made of tall dirt, and all the soldiers you see here live behind those dirt walls. The walls are there to keep the Confederate troops from taking the fort away from us."

"So it's like a village?"

"I would liken it to a village of sorts," he replied. "Just wait. You'll see for yourself in a few days."

Chapter 14

Big Forest Campground

Matt, Sarah and Sean walked up to Frank Willis' camper and Sean pulled out his digital camera and started taking pictures of the exterior from all angles. While Sean clicked away, Matt and Sarah checked the front door and all the windows.

"No signs of forced entry. Let's see what we've got inside," Matt said.

They slipped on disposable protective boots and hair nets and snapped on latex gloves, standard operating procedure to prevent any contamination of evidence. Matt noted in his notebook that Sean, Sarah and he accessed the camper with the date and time they entered it. *No mistakes on this one. Let's be sure to keep a tight chain on this - just in case it goes to trial.*

Sean entered first, snapping away with his digital camera. It was his job to record, in pictures, the way Willis' camper looked upon first entry. Not only would he photograph it when they entered, but he would take pictures of how it looked when they left. That way no one could accuse them of altering anything.

"Okay," he called out. "You guys can come in."

Matt and Sarah ducked under the yellow tape and entered the camper. The smell rushed to greet them.

Sarah gasped. "Whew, you'd think the guy died in here instead of the pool." She quickly scanned the interior. "And he didn't win any awards for neatness either." Newspapers, empty beer cans, old magazines, frayed area rugs and dozens of dust bunnies smothered the floor.

Sean continued to snap pictures as they carefully navigated through the domestic mine field to the kitchen table where they found a laptop computer, a cell phone, an empty beer can and two radios, one a citizen's band, the other a ham. Matt checked the dials on both radios to determine what frequencies Willis was using.

"Sean, get pics of these dials." It might not mean much, but since no one really knew much about the man, it could give them a picture of the kind of person Frank Willis was. Who was he talking to? Was it just a hobby? Or was something else going on? Nothing can be taken for granted when searching for evidence.

"Man, this guy was something else. I'll bag the beer can and computer and the cell, Matt," Sean said. "We might find something interesting."

Matt noticed a cork board nailed loosely to the wall in the tiny space that was considered the "living room area" of the small camper. "Check this out," he said. He reached up and removed an envelope that was pinned to the cork board. He flipped it open and removed a small piece of paper. "Huh, it's a two hundred dollar gift certificate to an electronics store, but it's expired. And look at this one." He pulled another envelope from the board and opened it. "Round trip tickets to the Bahamas…also expired. Odd."

"Maybe the guy didn't have anyone to go with," Sean smiled, snapping photos of every item on the board.

"Ya think?" Matt laughed. "But it's still weird. Let's bag this stuff, too."

"Right."

The investigators continued through the disaster known as home to the late Frank Willis.

"Well, I don't think the guy was into porn," Sarah said rummaging through Willis' stack of DVD's. "All I find are Westerns and war stuff."

Matt slid along the wall next to the bed and opened the night stand drawer. "I found his wallet. Don't see anything else," he said and handed the wallet to Sean, who placed it in a plastic bag.

Sarah found a TV guide dated June 2005 on the sofa, and then checked the drawers in the kitchen where she found a small personal phone book. "Let's bag this, too. Might be a relative in here we can contact. My guess is it doesn't look like anything happened here. I don't see signs of a struggle, but how can you tell? It all looks pretty normal for the bottom of a dumpster."

She turned to Matt. "Are you gonna need a ride back to the station when we're done with interviews?"

"Yeah, that would be great," Mat said.

She wrinkled her nose. "Please tell me we're done in here."

Matt called out to Sean. "Sean, you ready to get out of here?"

Sean sealed the bag containing the personal phone book and dropped it into his evidence collection box and closed it. "I think I've got what we need. Let's put a seal on it. My eyes are starting to water."

Matt looked down at the list of names in his notebook. *Look at this. Twelve I need to talk to...plus I have to get Julie's statement. I'll never get done. Glad Sarah's here to help.*

Police procedure dictated that interviews were to be conducted one-on-one. Matt knew from experience that someone sitting alone and feeling comfortable and relatively safe would likely say more than if they were sitting with another person or a group. After all, what if the interviewee had first-hand knowledge or a suspicion of "who-done-it", but was afraid to speak up because that person was sitting right next to them? Best to keep interviews in their purest form – that being singular.

Donna and Phil O'Neal's blue and white motor home sat about a hundred feet from the office on a large site reserved for the campground manager. She and Phil, along with their son Eric and Sonny, the maintenance man, were sitting outside when Matt arrived.

"Coffee?" Donna asked. "Just brewed."

"You know, that sounds good. I take mine black."

While Donna went inside the motor home to fetch a cup of coffee, Matt reached into his shirt pocket and pulled out a pen.

Donna returned and placed the coffee on a small plastic TV tray. "We're all in shock over this."

"I can imagine," Matt replied. "Like I told you earlier, I need to interview everyone in the park, including the four of you."

"What would you like to know?" Phil asked.

"If you don't mind, I'd like to get Sonny's statement first, since he discovered the body."

Matt looked at Donna. "Can we use your office? It's policy to conduct the interviews separately."

Donna nodded. "No problem. The door's open."

Matt grabbed his coffee cup, and he and Sonny headed for the office. Once inside the tiny area, Matt pulled a couple of chairs together, and he and Sonny sat face to face.

"I know you were pretty upset when I got to the pool area this morning, but I guess that's understandable."

"Damn right. That's the first dead person I've ever seen - except for…you know…funerals."

"Are you up for a few questions?" Matt asked trying to put Sonny more at ease.

Sonny, still shaken from the gruesome find, took a deep breath and nodded. "Okay."

"First I'll need your full name and address, your birth date, along with a phone number where you can be reached. As a matter of fact, if you have a driver's license, that will give me a lot of the stuff I need."

Sonny sucked nervously on his cigarette and blew a big puff; the smoke spiraled lazily upward. He reached into his hip pocket, pulled out his worn billfold, and handed Matt his license.

"So your name is Buford Lee Wallace and I see your address is listed as Bentwood, Mississippi," Matt said. "Is that where you live now?"

"No. I live here at the park. Bentwood's my home town, but I don't have a place there anymore. I sort of move around and do odd jobs," Sonny said.

"How long have you lived here at the park?"

"Almost a year," Sonny said.

Matt jotted the information in his book along with a reminder...*verify Mississippi address*.

"How about a phone number."

Sonny said, "It's my cell, but you can reach me on it twenty-four, seven."

Matt noted the phone number next to Sonny's name and flipped to a new page in his book.

"Why don't you start from when you got up this morning? Did you notice anything unusual then?" Matt asked. He didn't think Sonny was a likely suspect, but he didn't know the man. It was too early in the investigation to look past him. Besides, some criminals will try to throw suspicion off of themselves by feigning innocence and miraculously being the first one at the scene of the crime.

Sonny took a deep breath. "No, nothin' unusual. I had breakfast and went to start my chores. I've got a lot to do today. When I came around the corner by the tool shed...jees, I almost stepped in his blood. Then I saw a trail of it headin' for the pool, so I followed it."

"I noticed the gate to the pool was open. Did you open it?" Matt asked, scrawling notes as he went.

"No, it was already that way. I thought that was pretty odd, too. I mean, I always make sure I close it every night. That's when I started to freak out, so I headed to the edge of the pool, and I saw Frank. I mean...I didn't know it was Frank right then, but when I looked closer, I saw it was him. He was floatin' face down and the water around him was all red. Man, I ain't never seen anything like that before, and I never want to see it again," Sonny said and ran his fingers through his hair, hoping this was all just a bad dream.

"Did you know Frank?"

Matt's casual attitude was rubbing off on Sonny. The maintenance man relaxed and reached into his shirt pocket for a cigarette. "Well, not real personal-like. We never sat next to each other at the bar or anything like that. But I've seen him around," Sonny said and lit the cigarette.

"So you're saying Wilson drank?"

"I don't know that for sure. It was just a figure of speech. I ain't never seen him in the bars that I go to, that's all I'm sayin'."

"Did you see him last night?"

Sonny said, "No. Can't say as I did. Really, about the only time I see him is sometimes when he's headin' for his camper and I'm headin' for work. Real early in the morning. Sometimes before daylight."

"Some people say Willis was weird, spooky. You agree with that?" Matt asked, looking for a reaction.

Sonny, more relaxed now, shrugged his shoulders and nodded. "Sure…he was weird, but so what?"

"Did that bother you at all?"

"Me? Hell, no. Frank never bothered me. I don't think we spoke but ten words in all the time I've been here. After all, ain't we all just a little weird?"

Matt had to agree with Sonny on that one. He took a sip of his coffee. "Were you here at the park last night?"

Sonny suddenly stiffened. "If it's all the same with you, I'd rather not say."

"It would really help me out a lot if I knew your whereabouts last night, Sonny. You know, if it's embarrassing or something like that, I assure you, if at all possible, I'll keep it out of the report. It's in your best interest, too. It's just standard procedure. You know how that is."

"Well then," Sonny hesitated slightly. "I wasn't here. I was with a…certain lady." He took a draw on his cigarette in an attempt to hide an impish grin.

"And where was that?"

"At her house in Donaphan."

"How long were you with her?" Matt asked.

"Oh, I'd say I got there around ten last night and left about four this morning. Got home about four thirty, I guess. Washed my face, brushed my teeth and sat down to watch a little TV. Next thing I know the alarm's goin' off."

"Did you see anything unusual when you got back to the campground?"

Sonny thought briefly, then shook his head. "No. It was all quiet."

"I'll need the lady's name and her phone number," Matt said.

"You will?"

"Yes, I'll need to confirm that you were with her."

"Well, that might be a little dicey," Sonny smiled. "Ya see, she's got a husband *and* a boyfriend, and neither one of 'em know about...me."

Matt said, "I'll be sure and keep it discreet."

Sonny relented and gave Matt the woman's name and phone number. "She'll tell you I was there." He took another deep draw from his cigarette and let his mind wander back to the previous evening and its many pleasures.

Matt noted his book...*Check alibi and get T.O.D. to match.* If the time of death was after four thirty, that meant that Sonny would have had enough time to drive the short distance from Donaphan to the campground and possibly do Frank in. Though nothing Sonny had said led Matt to believe the maintenance man had anything to do with Frank's death, he couldn't rule out Sonny as a candidate – not just yet.

"Look, that's all I know. Can I get to work now? I've got a lot to do around here," Sonny said, crushing his cigarette in a nearby ashtray.

Matt looked up from his scribbles. "Sure. Thanks for your time. And if you think of anything else, please come by my camper."

Sonny smiled and then scrambled out of his chair on his way to his first assignment.

Matt grabbed his half-empty coffee cup and walked back over to the O'Neal motor home. There would be no one-on-one with young Eric O'Neal. Matt knew Eric had special needs, and that meant that the interview would be conducted with one of Eric's parents present. Donna, Phil and Eric were still sitting outside, waiting.

"Thanks for the use of the office," Matt said and sat down in a nearby lawn chair.

"You're welcome," Donna replied.

He flipped over another page in his book and said, "Okay, I'll do the same drill with all three of you. I need to get your names and birth dates. If you have driver's licenses, that will help."

"They're inside," Donna said and hopped up from her chair and hurried into the motor home. She reemerged with hers and Phil's licenses and handed them to Matt. He copied the information into his black book before returning them to her.

"I know you're full timers, but I need a phone number where I can contact you."

"Would this help?" Eric asked and produced a business card.

Matt looked at the brightly-colored card and smiled. "This is a neat idea, Eric. Did you do this?"

Eric nodded sheepishly. "Mom helped me do it on the computer. She says it saves...time. Just give people the card and...it has everything on it. Sometimes I forget my mom's cell phone number."

"Well, you did a great job on it. May I keep this?"

"Sure," Eric grinned.

Matt placed the card in his shirt pocket and turned his attention back to Donna and Phil. "I'd like it if one of the two of you were here with Eric during his interview. If you both want to be here, that's okay, too."

Phil hopped up and said, "Donna can do that. I'm gonna see if Sonny needs any help. I'll be back in a little while."

Once Phil was gone, Matt flipped to a new page in his notebook. "Did either of you see or hear anything last night?"

Donna said, "I can't speak for the guys, but I didn't. I went to bed about eleven and got up about five. I went to the office around five thirty and put on a pot of coffee."

Matt made notes in his book. "And you didn't see anything on your way to the office?"

"No. I'm not really a morning person, so I just kind of move in a fog until I get my first cup of coffee. It was still a little dark out, too."

"So you made the coffee. And then what?"

"I fired up the computer to see if I had any e-mails. I was reading one when I heard Sonny scream. I ran outside and saw Sonny standing in the pool...next to...Frank. I almost threw up. What in the world happened?"

"We're just starting our investigation, so I don't have much information right now," Matt said.

"I heard something," Eric blurted out.

"What did you hear, Eric?" Matt asked.

"It was...it sounded like somebody digging in the dirt."

"Digging?"

"Yeah, like with a...big...shovel or something like that. Like...scoop, scoop. You know...digging."

"Did you hear any motors or just the shovel hitting the dirt?"

"No motors." Eric shook his head.

Matt scribbled in his notebook. "Do you remember what time that was when you heard it?"

"Uh...it was later than when Mom and Dad went to bed. I was in bed, too. But I was looking out my window...watching the stars move. Did you know stars move?"

Matt nodded. "Yes, I did. But Eric, how much later? Do you remember?"

Eric furrowed his brow and squinted, trying to coax a memory. "No. I just know it was after Mom and Dad went to bed."

Matt noted Eric's comments. "Could you tell from the sound which way the digging was coming from?"

Eric shrugged his shoulders and shook his head. "No. Just outside somewhere."

"That's okay, Eric. You've given me some very important information. Thanks."

Matt looked at Donna. "Did you know Frank Willis?"

"Only as a resident of the park," Donna said. "I guess I'd call him a loner. I never saw him outside during the day. He slipped his lot rent through the night slot every month, after the office closed. I'm sorry, but I just don't know what else I can tell you."

Matt closed his notebook. "Thanks for the coffee. If I need anything further, I'll be in touch."

He found Phil raking the sand in the horseshoe pits and decided it was as good a place as any for the interview.

Phil wasn't much help. "Sorry, I really didn't hear anything. I had a busy day yesterday and when my head hit the pillow…that's all she wrote. I don't remember any strange noises. Nothing. And if Donna didn't post Willis' lot rent payment each month, we'd never know anybody lived there."

Matt thanked Phil and walked back toward the campground. He glanced at his notes as he walked…*No motive at this time. Barely knew victim. Son, Eric heard digging sound outside. Check for evidence of digging. NOTE: Get Junior Police badge for Eric.*

Matt walked up to site eleven, the Maynard's. John Maynard stepped out of his camper and shook Matt's hand. The two men then entered the Maynard camper.

"Please, sit down. Would you like some coffee?" John asked.

"Yes, I'd love some, thanks. My day started pretty early," Matt replied

Rose fetched a cup from the cabinet, poured it full of the steaming hot liquid and placed it on the table.

"Sugar or cream? How about a nice cinnamon roll?"

"Black is fine. I'll pass on the roll, but thanks." The aroma of freshly brewed coffee was irresistible. He needed as much caffeine as he could get right about now; interviews took a lot of energy. John sat across from him while Rose retreated to the sofa. John leaned forward and put both arms on the edge of the dining table.

"Frank Willis was found dead this morning," Matt said.

"Your wife and sister told us. What happened?" John asked.

"We don't have all the details yet, but I'd like to ask each of you some questions, if I may."

"Sure, fire away."

"First off, I need your full names."

"John Anderson Maynard and Rose Marie Maynard."

Matt scratched the names in his little black book. "Date of birth."

"I'm okay with givin' you mine," John said. "But you're on your own with Rose over there. You know how they are about givin' out that kind of information. Mine's October 26, 1939."

Rose rolled her eyes and shook her head. "See what I have to live with? My birthday is April 12, 1941."

Matt noted the dates. "You're from Wyoming, right?"

"Yes, a small town near Cheyenne called Horse Creek. We had a cattle ranch there for, oh, I don't know, probably thirty years. About ten thousand acres."

"That's a pretty big spread."

"I know. Too big when you get to be our age."

"What is your address in Horse Creek?"

"Well, we're full timers now. We don't really have one."

Matt thought back to Eric. "You wouldn't by any chance have a business card, would you?"

"Sure do," John said and pulled one out of his wallet.

Matt thanked him and put the card in his shirt pocket with the O'Neal family card, and then asked John if he would accompany him outside for a few minutes so they could talk. They both took their coffee and plopped down at a nearby picnic table.

"Did you know Frank Willis?" Matt asked.

"Nope, never laid eyes on the man."

Matt sipped his coffee and made notes in his notebook.

"Did you see or hear anything last night or early this morning?"

"Can't say as I did. I hear he was pretty weird."

"How so?" Matt asked.

"You heard what Stan Yates said. The guy was up in that old rust bucket all day, only goin' out after dark. Ya know, where I'm from, some people actually get scared of folks that don't act like everybody else. Then they begin to hate 'em. And that's a recipe for somethin' bad to happen." Matt knew exactly what John was talking about, phobias that lead people to hate others for the color of their skin, their sexual orientation or religion. He couldn't dismiss it as a possible motive.

"Do you hate people who are different than you?"

"Me? Heck, no. When you have a business like mine, you have to accept pretty much anybody who comes lookin' for work. And believe me, I've had some pretty odd ducks work for me. I remember this one guy...he wouldn't eat meals with the rest of us. Ate over behind the barn or somewhere where nobody'd see him. Now, we thought that a little odd until we found out he had to take his teeth out when he ate," John laughed. "But I sure didn't want to kill him because his dentures didn't fit. He was the best when it came to workin' cattle. How'd the old guy die, anyway?"

"We're not sure just yet. We're still in the initial phase of our investigation. I'll know more once I get the autopsy results."

"Darn shame. Anything else I can help you with?"

"Not right now, thanks. But could you ask Rose to come out for a few minutes? I'd like to get her statement."

"Sure thing," John said. "Hey Ro. There's a man out here to see ya."

He looked at Matt. "I'm gonna go round back and empty the gray tank while you talk to Rose. That okay?"

"Thanks, John," Matt said.

Rose stuck her head out of the camper. "More coffee?"

Matt smiled. "That would be great."

Rose filled his cup, and then sat down across from him in the bright sunlight. "What can I do for you?"

"Did you see or hear anything last night?" he asked.

Rose leaned forward. "No, we came back from the little concert down at the pavilion and sat outside for a few minutes. It was such a beautiful night. Then we came inside and watched TV for a while before we went to bed. I normally sleep light, but I must have been really tired. The last thing I remember was my head hittin' the pillow."

Several minutes later Matt closed his notebook and pushed his coffee cup over to Rose. "Thanks for the coffee. It was delicious."

"You're welcome," she replied. "Sure I can't get you a cinnamon roll?"

"I'll take a rain check on that."

John returned from behind the camper and stood behind Rose. "That it?" he asked.

"I think so, John," Matt said. "But if you think of anything else, please contact me. Here's my card, or if you see me across the street, feel free to come on over. You're free to leave anytime you like. Thanks for your time."

John nodded. "You're welcome. But we're not planning on leavin' any time soon so we'll be here if you need us. Hope you find whoever did this."

Matt left John and Rose and walked to the Yates' fifth wheel next door. He scribbled in his note pad...*No motive to murder Willis. Retired cattle ranchers. Check into possible hate crime.*

Stan and Lois were inside, finishing breakfast. "Please come in, Matt," Stan said. "Coffee? Tea? Lois drinks tea."

"I'll have coffee, black, if you don't mind."

"Not at all. Lois, honey, will you get Matt a cup of coffee? She can whip you up some breakfast if you'd like."

"No thanks. Coffee's fine." Matt's stomach was growling, but that would have to wait.

Stan and Matt sat outside under the awning in a couple of webbed chairs; Matt flipped his notebook to a blank page.

Stan took a big swig of coffee and asked, "So Frank Willis is dead? Do you know what happened?"

"No, not yet. It's still early in our investigation. I'd like to ask you a few questions."

"Shoot."

"Where do you folks live?"

"We live in Thomasville, just up the road a bit. Do you need the address?"

"Yes."

"It's 59752 South Tower Road, Thomasville."

"I'm familiar with Thomasville. Nice town. Have you lived there all your life?"

"No, we're originally from New York." He quickly held up his right hand. "I know, I know, we don't have that New York accent. We're not from the city. We lived north of Watertown, in Degrasse. It's a little town on the Grass River. Lots of good fishing and hunting up there."

"When did you move to Thomasville?"

Stan said, "After our daughter was…after she died, we decided we needed a change of scenery."

"And when was that?" Matt asked.

Stan didn't hesitate. "She died twelve years and three months ago. We stayed in Degrasse for a while, but moved here about ten years ago. I started up the guide business and Lois is my assistant. She takes calls and does the books. We do okay."

"Did you know Frank Willis?"

"No, not really. Just got a look at his camper, if you can call it that. We come here several times a year, and I'd say he's been living here for about a year now."

"Did you see or hear anything last night?"

"No, I didn't," Stan said. "I watched a little TV, then went to bed."

Matt jotted down in his little memo book…*Couple lives in nearby Thomasville. Daughter murdered twelve years three months ago.*

Once Matt finished getting Stan's statement, he went inside the camper to interview Lois.

"Sorry, no," Lois replied. "We got home from the concert and I went to bed and read a book. That usually puts me to sleep right away."

Matt noticed a photo sitting in the window sill. It showed Stan and Lois, along with a young girl. They were standing by a stream, and she was proudly holding up a trout for all to see.

"Is this your daughter?" he asked.

She smiled sadly. "Yes."

"I see she was a fisher, too."

"Like her dad," Lois replied and seemed to be lost in a brief memory.

Matt completed his interview and stepped outside the camper, followed closely by Lois. He had seen a lot in his years on the police force, and, like most people who are involved with the good as well as the bad side of humanity, thought he was pretty good at shutting out his emotions. But the human part of him couldn't help but silently grieve along with the couple who had lost their only daughter to a senseless crime. "Thanks for taking time to answer my questions and for the coffee. If you think of anything else, here's my card. Or just walk across the street."

"Yeah, we know where you live," Stan laughed.

Next stop on his list was site number twenty one, the Pettyjohns'. Matt knocked on the door of the camper, and Carolyn stepped out. "Please come in. Can I offer you some coffee?"

"I've had a couple already this morning, but I could use another, thanks. Black, please."

"Tom," Carolyn called. "Matt Baker is here."

Tom Pettyjohn opened the bedroom door and walked down the hall. They shook hands and Tom motioned for Matt to take a seat at the breakfast table.

"What can we do for you Matt?"

"Frank Willis was found dead this morning. I'm with the Alton police department and I've been assigned to the case. We're interviewing everyone in the park to see if they saw or heard anything last night. I'd like to get statements from both of you."

Carolyn poured Matt a cup of coffee and then grabbed her purse and walked to the door. "Do you want to talk to us together?"

"Actually, I'd like to talk to your husband first, then I can get your statement."

"Good. Then I'll run to the office and pay our lot rent. I'll be right back." She sprinted out the door, leaving the two men alone.

"Frank Willis? Huh. Well, Carolyn and I came back from the concert and went right to bed," Tom said. Matt was struck by Tom's obvious lack of concern.

"So you didn't see or hear anything?" Matt asked.

"Nope."

"Did you know Frank Willis?"

"Actually, this is our first time at this campground, so the answer to your question is no. Didn't want to know him either," Tom said.

"Why's that?"

"From what I hear the guy's spooky. Too much hidin' and sneakin' around at night for me. Saw too much of that in Nam."

"How many tours did you do?"

"One was enough. So, no offense, but I didn't want to have anything to do with him."

Matt noted his book...*Vietnam vet with combat experience. Doesn't like odd balls that sneak around at night.*

Tom stood. "Can we go fishing now?"

"Just a couple more questions. Are you employed?"

"Yeah, I'm an electrician. I work for Allied Electric in Cedar Rapids. Why?"

"Just curious, I guess. Do you have a home phone?"

"Yeah," Tom snorted and spat out his home phone number.

They were interrupted by Carolyn walking back into the camper. "Sorry, I forgot my checkbook."

"That's okay Mrs. Pettyjohn. I was just finishing up your husband's interview. If you have time we can do yours outside at the picnic table."

Tom glared. "Why do you want her to go outside?"

"I'd like to get her statement now."

"Why can't you do it right here?"

Matt said, "It's just procedure that we interview each person individually."

Rule number 1 in a cop's world – *keep control of the situation at all times. Never let things get out of your control.* If Matt relented and interviewed Carolyn where Tom wanted her to be interviewed, Matt would break rule number 1. And Matt was not about to relinquish control of this process to Tom Pettyjohn. "If this isn't a good time, I can come back. But I *will* have to have her statement before you two can leave the campground."

"Why? Are we suspects?" Tom shouted.

"Tom!" Carolyn snapped at him. "He's just doing his job. Let him do it." She placed her hand gently on his arm, and he seemed to relax slightly.

It was clear that Tom Pettyjohn didn't like being told what to do. He had endured enough of that during the war. But Matt had made it clear that he wanted to talk to Carolyn alone. He decided it wasn't in his best interest to cause a scene. Just get it over with. They'd done nothing wrong. "Then do what you gotta do. Give me the damned checkbook and I'll go pay the rent," he said and stomped off toward the office.

"Sorry about that," Carolyn said.

"That's okay," Matt said. "Did you know Mr. Willis?"

"No, I didn't."

"Did you ever see him around?"

"No," she said shaking her head.

"And do you work?"

"Yes, I work behind the counter at Felicia's Deli in Cedar Rapids. I'm not sure you can call it work, but that's what I do," she smiled.

"Did you hear or see anything unusual last night?"

Carolyn thought for a second. "No. We came back from the concert. I remember I went inside, called home to check on my folks and then went to bed."

"Well, thanks for your time. Both of you…enjoy your day on the water," Matt said and added another note to his memo pad…*Mr. has a short fuse.*

Hal Evans, a.k.a. Mr. Security, and his wife, Harriet were standing outside their camper when Matt arrived. He shook hands with both of them, and noticed that Hal immediately wiped his hands off on his blue jeans. *Guy's a germophobe, too.*

Harriet offered Matt a cup of coffee, but this time he declined.

"Mr. and Mrs. Evans, a man was found dead this morning."

Hal sat wide-eyed and speechless, wringing his hands.

"My goodness, who was it?" Harriet asked.

"His name was Frank Willis. He was a resident in the campground."

"Oh, how horrible. How can we help?"

"First, I need to get some personal information from both of you."

Matt repeated the name/address drill with Hal and Harriet, getting most of the information from Harriet.

He glanced up from his notebook. "I need to know if you saw or heard anything last night."

"No, we were inside all evening, weren't we Hal?"

Hal nodded, turned and walked to the camper and began to jiggle the door handles on several basement compartments.

"He's just a little nervous," Harriet said, smiling meekly.

"Did you know Mr. Willis?"

"Heavens, no, this is our first visit here. We're from Beech Grove, Indiana. Over near Indianapolis." Matt could hear the jiggling of door handles as Hal circled the motor home.

"My husband has a....slight condition," Harriet whispered. Matt nodded in agreement. So much for one-on-one interviews.

"Are either of you employed?"

"Hal is a computer technician for International Tech Group. His office is in Indianapolis. I stay home and sell stuff on Ebay." She leaned forward and softly said. "He's not crazy. He just needs to check things a lot."

"Well, thank you for your time. If you think of anything, something you might have seen or heard last night, please let me know." Matt handed Harriet his business card. She looked at it. "We sure will."

Matt noted his book...*Not strong suspects. Mr. has issues with door handles.*

Throughout the late morning and early afternoon Rachel and Julie watched as Matt methodically visited campers to conduct interviews. Around one thirty he stopped at the campsite for lunch. "Okay, I'm done with my interviews."

"How's it going?" Rachel asked.

"It's going. Sarah's taking the other six for me. Oh, and let me make some notes on what you saw last night, Julie."

"Yeah, that was really weird," Julie said.

"Want some lunch?" Rachel asked.

"That I do. I'm starved. But first, I gotta pee. Coffee's yellin' to get out."

Rachel went inside and returned with a turkey sandwich, some sliced red peppers and a bottle of water. Matt ate and jotted on his note pad...*Witness is detective Baker's sister. Saw unknown*

sub running toward hiking trail at 1:45 a.m.. Unsub was
carrying some kind of package. Unsub returned 10 minutes later
without package. Check trails for evidence.

"Okay, Julie. Read this and tell me if I have everything."

Julie scanned the notes. "Yeah, only one thing."

"What?"

"Your handwriting's terrible," she laughed and handed him the book.

He smirked. "Very funny. The crime scene personnel are here processing the pool, the parking lot and the rest of the campground. They should be taking the body to the pathologist for autopsy pretty soon. I'm almost sure it was a homicide. They had to use the pool skimmer to get some of his intestines."

Julie felt queasy. "Ooh, Matt, too much information. Did they find anything in the woods?"

"I don't think they've been over there yet. But don't worry, we'll search the area."

"Maybe I can help."

"I don't think so, sis. Can't let you do that. Official police business."

"Bummer."

"Yeah...bummer."

Matt sipped his water. "So far this one is a puzzler, but with possibilities. I can't rule out that it was a random murder, a crime of opportunity. The maintenance man says he has an alibi, which I still have to check. And the O'Neal's didn't hear anything. Except their son, Eric. He said he heard digging near their motor home, so I'm gonna get someone to check that out. The Maynard's didn't give any indication that either one of them had a motive to kill Willis. They're cattle ranchers. Stan and Lois Yates' daughter was murdered years ago, and Frank Willis lived in New Jersey and they lived in nearby New York. I'm not sure if there's any connection there. The Maynard's and the Yates' said they didn't see or hear anything last night. Mr. Security down there freaked out when I showed up. He was pretty nervous during the interview, but that could be just because he's a weirdo. His wife said they didn't hear anything. They were home all night and didn't go out of their camper. Imagine that! The Pettyjohn's just want to go fishing, but he did a tour of duty in Vietnam and doesn't like sneaky people. And he about jumped down my throat when I said I wanted to talk to his wife separately. Guy's a loose cannon."

He finished off his bottled water with one big swig. "Like I said, Sarah's going to take care of the Hancock's, Atwater's and the two in the van. When we're finished with all of this, I'll need to head back to the station. I may be late. Don't hold supper."

"Okay, hon. See you when you get back."

Chapter 15

Big Forest Campground

Sarah Nelson, Matt's partner on the Alton Police force, walked down to space twenty to interview Jerry and Trina Hancock. Their fifteen-foot camper, a pop-up, was white with forest green stripes along the sides and across the top. Folded up for transport, the camper looked like a cigar box, but ‚popped up' to provide space for cooking and sleeping. The air conditioning in a pop-up comes from the breeze that flows through the window screens, and with no furnace, cold weather camping is left to the hardy. Trina was sitting in a web-style recliner under the overhanging branches of a large oak tree and looked up when Sarah approached.

"Mrs. Hancock, I'm Detective Nelson of the Alton police department. Is your husband here, also?" Sarah asked.

"Sure. He's napping. Jerry! You're wanted out front."

"Coming," Jerry yawned as he stepped out of the pop-up to greet Sarah. "Sorry, we had an early morning, and I was catching up on my beauty sleep."

"Early morning?"

"Yeah, we were out trying to find the geo treasure hunt clue before anybody else."

Sarah knew something about geocaching. She did a little bit of it in her spare time. But she had never heard that term before. "Geo treasure hunt?"

"The official term is geo treasure hunting. The website is geotreasures.com. It's kind of like geocaching, but with lots more clues that take you to all kinds of different places and the prizes are bigger."

"Oh…so did you find what you were looking for?"

"Unfortunately, no. Somebody's a little richer this morning, but not us. Better luck next time," Jerry said sleepily.

"Richer?"

"Yeah, this treasure hunt was for the big bucks. Ten thousand."

"Wow. That's some serious cash. How early is early?" Sarah asked.

"We were up, oh, I don't know, what time was it Trina? About four thirty?"

"I guess so," Trina replied. "Why?"

Sarah made a notation in her book, and then looked up at the couple. "One of the residents of the campground, a man named Frank Willis was found dead in the pool this morning."

"Oh, no, that's awful," Trina said and quickly sat up in the recliner.

"I'd like to ask you both a few questions. Mr. Hancock, can you excuse your wife and me for a few minutes."

"Oh…sure. I need to hit the restroom, anyway," Jerry said.

"Then I'll get your statement when you get back," Sarah said.

Jerry trotted off toward the park restrooms, saying he would be back in about five minutes.

"What would you like to know?" Trina asked.

"Did you know Frank Willis?"

"No. This is our first time here, and we were only here because of the money," Trina said.

"Did you hear or see anything around the pool area last night or early this morning?" Sarah asked.

"No, can't say that I did. But I was too busy looking for the clue. Look, detective, we have to be out of here tomorrow. We're due back at work Friday evening. We can't be late for work."

"Where's work for you two?"

"We both work for Ace Security in Kansas City."

"I don't think I know that one," Sarah said.

"We use GPS to track and locate missing and stolen vehicles and notify the police when we find them. We work nights. That's why we have to be back by Friday night."

"I'm sure that won't be a problem."

After getting names and home and work addresses, Sarah honed in on the geo treasure hunt. "You said you missed out on the big bucks. Was the clue hidden near here?"

Trina said, "Yeah, if you go to the light pole next to the office, you'll find the hole. When we got there, it was just a mound of dirt. So we started to dig. When we got to the box and opened it, it was empty. And we found an empty beer can next to it. Apparently somebody thought that was funny."

Sarah entered the information into her book, and then flipped open her cell phone and dialed a number. "Ron. It's Sarah. Hey, get a tech and go over to the light pole next to the office. You'll see a hole that contains an empty box and an empty beer can. Have them bag it for evidence. Oh, and have them take a sample of the dirt, too."

She hung up the phone and turned her attention back to Trina. "Is there anything else you can remember?"

Trina shook her head. "No, that's about it. We came back here and tried to get some sleep."

Jerry returned from the restroom area, but wasn't able to offer any additional information.

"Thanks for your time," Sarah said. "If you think of anything you might have seen or heard, please contact me." She handed Jerry her business card.

"We sure will. We plan on staying over tonight and leaving tomorrow. Is that okay with you?"

"You're free to go anytime you want."

Sarah walked away and jotted a note in her book...*Check out geotreasures.com to see who won $10,000.*

Next, Sarah turned her attention to the camper occupied by Howard Kraft and Sheila Young. It was actually a 1970 Volkswagen van. The once white exterior paint was now a melody of rusty beige and brown resulting from years of neglect. Sheets of aluminum foil blanketed the inside of the front windshield, making a good curtain to block the sun's harsh rays, as well as prying eyes. Two metal folding chairs sat on the concrete patio and a pair of men's shorts hung from a piece of clothes line strung between the back of the van and a nearby small oak tree.

The couple sat outside at the picnic table eating chips and salsa and drinking beer.

"Hi. Want some?" Howard asked.

"No thanks," Sarah replied. "I'm Detective Nelson with the Alton police, and I'd like to ask you two some questions about last night, if you don't mind."

"Not at all. What happened?"

"Frank Willis' body was found in the park pool."

Howard appeared to be genuinely shocked. "What?"

"For the record, can I have your full names?" Sarah wrote the names of Howard and Sheila down, along with their cell phone numbers.

While Howard walked off toward the volleyball court, Sarah moved his empty beer can to one side and plopped her notebook down on the picnic table. "Were you here all night last night?" she asked Sheila.

"Yes. You see…Howard works nights. I just stay here at the camper until he gets home. Then we go to breakfast sometimes. I didn't see anything, though." Sheila's voice shook.

"Did you know Frank Willis?"

"Ya know, only to see him. He was a really strange guy, wanderin' around here all hours of the night," Sheila said. "Some nights I can't sleep cause it's too hot. I sit outside to cool off. That's when I see him."

"Did you see him last night?" Sarah asked.

"No. I watched reruns of Gilligan's Island on TV. Howard and I just love that show," she giggled. "That Gilligan, he's so funny."

When Howard returned, Sheila took the opportunity to walk to a nearby liquor store for more beer.

Sarah flipped to a new sheet in her notebook. "Do you work, Mr. Kraft?"

"Yeah, at the True Value down the road apiece. I stock shelves and clean the store. I work from eleven at night to seven in the morning," Howard replied.

"How do you get to work? I don't see a car, and you obviously don't drive your van."

"Oh, there's another guy I work with. He picks me up at the front gate, over by the office, and drops me off after work."

"What's his name?" Sarah asked, jotting in her notebook.

"Ryan. Ryan Ashmore. Real nice guy. Lives in Alton somewhere. I don't really know his address or anything."

"Did Ryan pick you up last night?"

"Sure. About ten forty-five or so. It's only a ten minute drive to the True Value, so he don't have to pick me up till it's almost time to go to work."

"What kind of car does Ryan have?"

"It's a Ford pickup truck. Blue...light blue."

"Does Ryan have a phone number?"

"Yeah. Let me get it for you." He crawled into the van, returning with a piece of paper. "I suppose you're gonna want to talk to him, huh?"

"Is that going to be a problem?"

"Nope. He'll tell ya I was there all night till quittin' time this morning."

"Did you know Frank Willis?" Sarah asked.

"No. Only to see him around sometimes. He wasn't real sociable."

"Well, If you remember anything, you can reach me at this number," Sarah said and handed Howard her card.

"Sure thing," Howard said.

Sarah walked away and one half of the Gilligan's Island fan club returned to the salsa and beer. She made several notes in her black book...*Contact Ryan Ashmore to confirm Howard's alibi. Howard works nights at True Value. Check for Gilligan's Island on TV last night.*

She walked up to the big luxury motor home of Ken and Lydia Atwater. The Atwater's were parked on a site reserved for handicapped campers that was located directly across from the showers and the pool. Handicapped sites differ from regular sites. They are built with concrete patios so wheelchairs and walkers can navigate smoothly and are wider than a regular site to accommodate vehicles with lifts or ramps. Site thirteen was no exception, spacious, with a large patio, a walkway and even a concrete sidewalk leading to the fire pit.

Sarah knocked on the coach door, and Ken stepped out to greet her.

"Good afternoon. I'm detective Nelson with the Alton police department," Sarah said.

"Mind if we talk outside? My wife's taking a nap," Ken said.

"No problem."

The two sat at the picnic table.

"This is a beautiful coach," Sarah said.

"Thanks," Ken replied.

"How big is this thing?"

"Forty feet."

"Diesel, I assume?"

"Yep. It's got all the bells and whistles."

"And a satellite dish, I see. That's nice."

"Yeah, especially for my wife, Lydia. She's in a wheel chair and chases stocks all over the globe. She can keep track of the market no matter where we are. What can I do for you detective?"

"A camper in the park by the name of Frank Willis was found dead this morning."

Ken squinted. "Willis? Which one was he?"

"He lived in an old camper toward the back of the campground."

Ken smiled and looked up toward the sky. "Well, I'm pleased to hear that."

Sarah was stunned. "What do you mean?"

"I have to tell you something, detective. I know Frank Willis. He's the man who crashed his car into my wife and caused her injuries ten years ago."

"Are you sure about that?"

"Yes, I'm sure."

"Then maybe you were out for a little revenge." Sarah said.

Ken sighed. "No, detective, I'm not out for revenge. But I'm not sorry he's dead, either. Lydia doesn't know about this...about Willis. He must have changed his name and moved from New Jersey to this area. We knew him as Arthur Hatcher. She didn't see him last night when we came back to the coach, but I did. I couldn't believe my eyes. And he saw me, too. I know that. He avoided looking, but I know he recognized us. He ran off toward that piece of junk of his. Frankly, his death just took a huge weight off my shoulders. I know that sounds horrible, but you don't know what it's like watching the one you love struggle with everyday activities, and know it's going to be like that for the rest of her life. I'd give anything if it was me in that chair and not her. I know it's not right to hate that much, and to be happy someone is dead. How did he die?"

"All we know right now is that he was found floating in the pool. We're still in the initial stages of the investigation."

"Huh. Well, even though I hated him, I'm telling you here and now that I had nothing to do with his death."

"Thanks for your honesty, Mr. Atwater, but I still need to know where you were last night."

"I was here, putting Lydia to bed. We watched a little TV and then both of us went to sleep. When she gets up from her nap, you're welcome to ask her. I just beg you not to tell her that Willis was Hatcher." His eyes pleaded for understanding.

"Not unless it's absolutely necessary," Sarah said.

Before Sarah left, she got Ken and Lydia's personal information and a can-be-reached phone number. She was intrigued by Ken's statement and wanted to be sure she could reach him again...just in case.

"Thank you," Ken said. They shook hands and Sarah walked back to the office area.

She scribbled in her notebook...*Knows vic. Vic used to be Arthur Hatcher. Shaky alibi. Mr. is glad Willis is dead. Still need to interview wife.*

She took out her cell phone and called Matt. "I'm done here, Matt. The Hancock's told me about digging up a spot near the office during a geo treasure hunt. I called a tech and had them retrieve any evidence."

"Really? The O'Neal kid heard digging last night. I bet it's the same spot. Thanks for getting that for me," Matt said.

"No problem. Need anything else from me?"

"Just that ride back to the station when we're done. Oh, and do you have a junior police badge in your Kid's Kit in your cruiser?"

"I'm sure I do. Why? Did you lose yours?" she laughed.

"Yuk, yuk. No, I want to give it to Eric O'Neal. What a great kid. I think he might like it."

"I'm on my way back to the office area. My car's right there. Maybe we can both present it to him."

"Yeah, he'd get a kick out of that!"

Chapter 16

December, 1864
Fort Davidson - near Pilot Knob, Missouri

The patrol, along with Francois, Victoria and Skunk made their way out of the dense forest and formed a single line as they approached Fort Davidson.

Corporal Wilson turned to his rider. "Well, Miss Victoria, we are almost to the fort. See it up ahead?"

Victoria leaned up and put her chin on his shoulder, but she saw nothing. "No."

"It's behind that big long hill there." A five foot tall dirt and grass hill stretched out before them.

Victoria laughed. "It looks like a very big mole has been here."

"Ya know, now that you say it, it does look like a big ole mole tunnel," Wilson said. "There are six of these big hills altogether, and they connect to each other and make a big area for us to stay in." A five foot deep dry moat, something attacking soldiers would have to run down into and then run up the opposing five foot high mole hill in an attempt to get inside the fort, surrounded the fort's perimeter. A wooden draw bridge spanned the moat; it was the only way in and out of the fort.

When they entered the fort, she saw several large cannons sitting next to the walls on man-made dirt platforms; each cannon seemed to be peaking out over the giant mole runs. "What are those?"

"Those are called cannons," Wilson said. "They are really big guns that shoot big bullets at Johnny Reb."

"At who?"

"Johnny Reb. That's what we call the Confederate soldiers that we're fightin'. We call 'em that because they're rebels and want to have their own country."

She looked around the interior of the fort and noticed a large mound of dirt approximately ten feet high in the center. "And what is that?"

"We call that a magazine. We keep all of our bullets and the powder for our guns and cannons in there."

"You mean under the ground?"

"Yep. That's our way of protecting our ammunition. If Johnny Reb comes calling and fires shells in here from outside, the shells will just hit the dirt and make big dents but won't set our powder ablaze and send us all to the Promised Land."

"But you said it was like a village. Mama said her village had many houses. I don't see any houses. What are those things?"

Wilson smiled. "Those are tents. That's what we live in. I guess you could call 'em houses, only we can take 'em down, put 'em on the back of our horses, and put 'em up elsewhere."

Victoria was overwhelmed with all the new terms she was hearing. Apparently soldiers had their own language – just like the Cherokee and the white man did.

Once all were safely inside the earthen walls of the fort, Sergeant Smith gave the orders. "Corporal Wilson, take Mr. Adams to one of the empty tents. And see if you can scare up some soap and water for him. He probably won't use it, but at least we offered. Stand guard until we conduct the court martial. If he tries to flee, shoot him. Mr. Levalier and Miss Victoria will accompany me to Major Jordan's tent."

"Yes sir," Wilson replied. He turned around to help Victoria dismount. "Good luck, little lady," he said and gently helped her down.

"Thank you for the ride, corporal," she replied with a big grin.

"It was indeed my pleasure, Miss Victoria."

Francois and Victoria followed the sergeant to the tent of Major Thomas Jordan, commander of the Union forces at the fort.

"This way, Mr. Levalier," Sergeant Smith said holding the tent flap open. Francois and Victoria stepped into the small, starkly furnished portable office.

"Major, sir, this is Mr. Francois Levalier and his niece, Miss Victoria Levalier. They are here to press charges against one William Adams. We know him as Skunk, sir. He's wanted for murder in the state of Missouri."

Major Jordan looked up from his papers. "Mr. Levalier, may I inquire as to how Mr. Adams wronged you?"

"He came on my brother's land, shot him in the back and stole his furs and his gun. My niece is now an orphan."

Jordan's eyebrows raised. "I see. And you saw him kill your brother?"

"*Non*, but he had my brother's pelts and his gun."

Victoria stepped toward Major Jordan. "And he told us he killed my papa because he was a Yankee."

Major Jordan smirked. "A story I've heard too many times already in this war. Sergeant, please have Private Livingston prepare the necessary documents for Mr. Levalier to sign. We will try Mr. Adams for murder and for being a bushwhacker."

The sergeant saluted his superior. "Yes sir."

Major Jordan turned back to Francois and asked, "How is it you came upon Skunk Adams, Mr. Levalier?"

"We tracked him from where we found my brother's body. He dragged the skins and left a good trail. And he had my brother's gun."

"Excellent. Then you will testify to that during the trial?"

Francois hesitated. "Trial? Here?"

Major Jordan stood up. "Chances are Adams is a soldier with the Confederate Army. My guess is he is also a deserter. Regardless of his loyalties, that makes him despicable in my eyes. But this is not a military matter, since he's not being tried for being a deserter. While this war continues, Fort Davidson is considered the area court for all matters, military or otherwise. So, I ask you again, sir, will you testify?"

"I will...we will," Francois said and put his arm around Victoria.

The Major turned to Sergeant Smith. "Sergeant, tell Corporal McDonald that he will be defending the accused, and Sergeant Meyer is to be informed that he will be prosecuting."

Sergeant Smith looked at Francois and Victoria. "I'll secure accommodations for you while you're here. These trials don't last very long."

"Thank you, Sergeant. You have been very kind," Francois said.

"The documents will be completed this afternoon, and we will file formal charges against Mr. William Adams. I will allow Corporal McDonald time to prepare a defense. The trial will commence tomorrow," Major Jordan said.

Francois and Victoria ate with the troops that evening, and bunked in a vacant tent, courtesy of Corporal Wilson, who bunked with someone else. Francois snored away, but Victoria couldn't sleep. She stepped outside and looked up at the glistening night sky.

Oh, Papa, this is so different. The soldiers...some kind of war where people try to hurt each other...this place. I'm not sure I want to be here. But I must tell them what I saw and heard.

The court martial began the following morning. Sergeant Curtis Meyer spent about fifteen minutes beforehand with Francois and Victoria preparing them for their testimony. "Now, you'll sit next to the lieutenant. And I'll inquire as to how you knew it was Adams who killed your brother. You must relate your story about how you tracked him and he had your brother's pelts and his gun. And Victoria, don't be afraid. You must share with the court about how Adams confessed to you and then lied to Sergeant Smith. Okay?"

Victoria looked at Meyer with wide eyes. "I'm not afraid."

When asked to testify, Victoria stood straight and tall; she pointed directly at Skunk Adams. "He said he killed my father and enjoyed doing it."

Skunk had no defense, and no alibi, but he ranted anyway. "This illegal army is killin' all the good southern men. It is my duty as a Confederate to kill as many Yanks as I can. I am a hero. The Confederacy will remember my name," he boasted. "And I know what y'all want. I'll not sign an oath of allegiance to the illegal union you call the United States of America. The Confederacy's the only legal government for me. I ain't doin' it!"

When arguments for the defense were finished, Major Jordan adjourned the court martial for several minutes to consider his verdict.

Upon his return Major Jordan read his decision. "It is the verdict of this court that the defendant, William Adams, also known as Skunk Adams, is guilty of being a bushwhacker and of the murder of Henri Levalier." He glared at Skunk. "Sir, you have taken a man's life. And I am quite convinced that you have taken many more. In addition, you have refused to sign an oath of allegiance to the United States of America. Therefore, the punishment for your crime is that you are to be executed by firing squad. Normally I would have you taken to Fort Gratiot and have you shot there, but I can't spare the men. Therefore, the sentence is to be carried out immediately. May God have mercy on your soul. Corporal, take the prisoner, and assemble a firing squad. Remove him to the woods and dispatch him to his maker."

"You can't kill me. I done the Confederacy a service! I'll kill all a ya! Ya hear me. All a ya!" Skunk screamed defiantly.

Two soldiers dragged him kicking and screaming out into the yard.

"Major, are we allowed to watch?" Francois asked.

"Do you desire that?"

Victoria spoke first. "Yes!"

Sergeant Smith knew how gruesome death by firing squad was. He knelt down next to her. "Miss Victoria, I don't think you should watch this. He will get his just rewards for killing your papa, but let it be just that. Why don't we go for a walk and you can tell me about your mama and papa and how you track animals."

Chapter 17

Big Forest Campground

While Matt and the others finished the initial investigation, Julie and Rachel had a light lunch of turkey and Swiss cheese roll-ups and iced tea.

"I'll do supper tonight," Julie said. "Matt told me to bring lots of lettuce, so I did."

"Okay, I've got a few peppers and cukes and we can slice some of this turkey and add it. But before we start to salivate too much, want to take a walk?"

"Sure, but can we talk about something other than dead people and murderers?"

"Done," Rachel replied.

The afternoon sun glowed white hot, both women donned ball caps to shade their eyes and slathered on the sun screen.

"As hot as it is and all the weight we're sweating off, we'd better plan to be in line two hours early at the ice cream social Sunday," Rachel said. "You know those seniors. Gotta be there to get all that hot fudge and whipped cream. Heaven help Donna if she runs out."

Julie was in the middle of a swig of water, and she laughed and dribbled it all down the front of her shirt. "Hey, now, I'm almost a senior. And I want some of that hot fudge."

"Right you are. And I'll let you in line ahead of me," Rachel laughed.

They slowed their pace under the shade of an old elm tree. Julie appreciated the slightest change of temperature.

"So, are you ready to move back closer to the big city?" Julie asked.

"Ya know, I never thought I would like small town living, but Alton is great. What a nice town! And I love my job," Rachel said.

"That's good. But I'm not so sure I could do without my Starbuck's."

"What? You think we don't have all the amenities in Alton?"

"You have a Starbuck's?"

"Nope. We've got something better. The Filling Station on the Square. They have the best coffee around. And cheaper than Starbuck's, too. And there's this neat little place over on Market Street called The Lunch Box. Their turkey on whole wheat is to-die-for! We should go there one day this week. Matt may be busy for a while with this investigation."

"Okay. I'm always up for food. Jeez, I've gotta stop that." Julie smacked herself in the head with the palm of her hand.

"Look, you can't starve yourself and expect to lose weight. That's not the way to body works. You have to feed it, but you have to feed it right. Stick with me and you'll see that pants size go down."

"Okay, you're the pro."

The two women eased out into the bright sunshine again. "Got any plans for the summer?" Rachel asked.

"If it stays this hot, I'll be in the air conditioning doing family tree stuff."

"I thought you were done with that."

"Oh, I wish. I hit a brick wall with my great-grandmother, Victoria, and decided to put it up for a while. But I think I'm ready to pick it back up again. I *did* discover that she lived in the

Graniteville area, and I got her marriage license, and death certificate. But I still don't know where she's buried. I tell you, Rach, if you have any desire to trace your ancestry, get as much as you can from relatives. Take pictures. Do video interviews, anything you can while they're alive. Because once they're gone, you've lost all that history. I wish I had asked my mom more about her side of the family. Now I have so little to go on."

"What are you gonna do now?" Rachel asked.

"I don't know. I'm open to suggestions," Julie said.

"Well, maybe you could go to a genealogy club meeting. Check with the library when you get back home. I think that's where they meet."

"Yeah, my friend, Bev said the same thing. It would be so cool to find out more about Victoria, wouldn't it? Even if I knew where she was buried or if she really was Cherokee Indian."

"Yeah, that would be cool," Rachel said. "You know, they say that if you speak the name of a person who has passed away that their spirit will draw near to you."

"Who says that?" Julie asked.

Rachel shrugged. "I don't know. I've just heard that somewhere. Probably from one of the old timers at the clinic. You should say her name more. Maybe she'll show up and fill in the gaps."

"Well, it can't hurt," Julie said. She cupped her hands over her mouth and called out. "Yo, Victoria, if you're out there somewhere, I'm looking for you."

They walked and talked about things like jobs, kids, neighbors – anything but Frank Willis.

"Mike has been giving me grief about this Victoria thing," Julie said.

"Why?" Rachel asked sipping her water.

"I don't know. Thirty years of marriage. I love him to death, but sometimes I just want to choke him."

"You met him in college, didn't you?"

"I was in college. He was the mechanic Dad called to fix my car. He was eye candy, to say the least," she smiled. "Those pecs, and that nice tight butt. And I love mussing up his hair. Oops, sorry. Is that too much info?"

"Nah. It's just us girls here," Rachel replied.

"And he still looks great to me. That's why I'm here. I want to get back to my size seven pants. Mike says it doesn't matter to him, but I just feel my youth slipping away. Not slipping...more like flying!"

"It's supposed to slip away, Julie. But they say you should accept it and grow old gracefully."

"There you go with *they say* again. Well, I don't care what *they say*. I'm goin' kickin' and screamin'."

On their fourth lap around the park Julie was tired and hot. "Time out. I need a rest."

"Okay, we'll call it quits for a while. I think we burned off a few calories. I've got bottled lemonade in the fridge. Want one?"

"Sounds good. I'm headin' for that chair," Julie said and staggered to the lounge chair on the patio. "What time is it, anyway?"

"I think it's about four thirty," Rachel replied.

Rachel hopped into the camper and returned with two bottles of lemonade, handing one to Julie; she twisted the cap and took a swig. "Okay, here's the plan. When I finish this, I'll go get a shower and then make a big salad. We can eat here, if that's okay with you."

"Sure. I've got the turkey and the veggies. Oh, and I have some wine. And I'll bring the laptop so we can check out that website. They have WiFi here. What do ya say, about six thirty?"

"Sounds like a plan. Want to do a campfire tonight?" Julie asked.

"Sure, why not. Matt took the time to get the wood. Might as well use it."

They ate supper, and talked mostly about diets and exercises and weight lifting programs. After supper Rachel fired up the laptop and the two women looked up the geotreasures website. Visitors to the site could click on a number of options:

- *Home*
- *Previous treasure hunts*
- *Hunt Winners*
- *Prizes*
- *Chat Room*

Rachel looked at Julie. "Well, which one do we want?"

"Let's try *prizes*. That's where the big bucks should be."

Rachel clicked on the button and up popped a screen listing prizes that had been awarded during the last twelve treasure hunts.

Julie scanned the list. "These prizes aren't too bad. Look. There are cruise tickets, restaurant coupons, oil changes for life. And here it is; the grand prize for the current treasure hunt is ten thousand dollars. He was right."

"Man, what a sweet deal. No wonder people get caught up in this. See what *Hunt Winners* says." Rachel clicked on the button and displayed the previous twelve winners.

"It looks like people use code names. There are some funny ones here," Julie said. "S-HOLMES, that's cute. ITISMINE, now that's original. That name is shown five different times. Man, he's won a lot of stuff. QUESTNERD, yeah, I'll bet he's a nerd. How about this one...WANTITALL. Or this one...FINDEM. Creative, huh?"

"Okay. What would your name be?" Julie asked.

Rachel thought for a moment. "Oh. I don't know. Maybe something like...um...GOLDDIGGER."

"Ooh," Julie said. "You'd fit right in. I'd probably go with DIGGINIT."

"That's cute, too," Rachel said.

They finished looking at the other areas of the website, and Rachel shut down the computer.

"Well, that was interesting," Rachel said. "Maybe you should be a treasure hunter during your summer breaks."

"Yeah, I'll put that at the top of my list," Julie laughed. With the sun setting, they took their wine and moved outside by the fire pit. Rachel lit the teepee of twigs Matt had made for them the previous day, and added larger sticks and logs until the fire was fully ablaze. They sat quietly in the lounge chairs and welcomed the mild summer evening.

From across the street John Maynard called out, "Mind if we join you?"

"Not at all, come on over," Rachel yelled back.

John and Rose crossed Robin's Nest Lane and approached the women.

"We were hopin' you'd light this thing tonight. We brought chairs," he said.

"And some marshmallows, if anybody wants some," Rose added. The four sat under the brilliant summer sky, and soon talk turned to events of the day.

"Any more on Frank?" John asked.

"No, Matt's at the police station now," Rachel replied.

"Just awful," Rose said, shaking her head.

"Hey, you folks eatin' marshmallows without me?" Stan Yates shouted from across the street.

"Well get your butt over here and I'll roast you one," Rose called back.

"Just one?" he laughed, stepping from the shadows into the fire's welcoming light.

"Where's Lois?"

"She's comin'. Hey hon, bring some lawn chairs."

"Be right there," Lois called.

John looked up at Stan. "Did you catch any fish today?"

"Not many. I did get a few crappie. Boy, that's a good eatin' fish. And I hooked into a good sized catfish."

"Yes, but he threw it back," Lois interjected lugging two lawn chairs and a cooler filled with beer. "He's lost his boning knife."

Stan reached over and took the cooler from her and sat it on the ground. "It's not lost. I probably left it somewhere in the camper. I'll find it."

"Well, as long as it is, it shouldn't be too hard to find. I just hope you didn't drop it between the cushions in the couch. That would be an interesting story to tell them at the emergency room, wouldn't it?"

"Why don't you just give me one of those chairs," Stan snorted.

The fire seemed to melt away the tension, and the group was content to roast marshmallows. Each felt a kinship to the others and would forever be connected to the events surrounding the death of Frank Willis.

"I'll be glad when this fiasco is over and we can get back to something that feels normal," Rose said.

"Yeah, nobody deserved to die like that," Julie replied.

"Oh, I disagree with you." The voice came from the darkness behind Julie's RV.

"Why?" Rachel asked straining to see. Ken Atwater strode out of the black night. "He's the one who hit Lydia."

"Are you sure?" John asked.

"You don't think I'd remember the face of the son of a bitch who put my wife in a wheelchair for the rest of her life? Hell yes it was him."

"When did you see him?"

"Last night, after we left the bon fire over at the pavilion. He was walking to the dumpster with his trash, I guess. He saw me and got outta there in a hurry. Lydia didn't see his face, thank God. And I would appreciate it if you all kept this to yourselves. I told the police what I saw, so I'm not hiding anything – except from Lydia. I know I should feel guilty for being happy about his death, but I'm not. I'm glad he's dead, but I didn't do it."

He stood staring at the flames stretching upward trying to tickle the night sky.

Rachel broke the silence. "What will you do now?"

"I think I'll go golfing tomorrow." He thought for a brief moment. "You know, Lydia forgave Frank a long time ago. She's accepted her situation and made the best of her life. And me...what have I done? I've wasted a lot of my life hating the guy for what he did to her. That's gotta stop. Goodnight, everyone," he said and turned and drifted back into the ebony night.

Silence smothered the campers. Finally John spoke. "What was that all about?"

Rachel looked at the group. "I don't know. Maybe he just needed to tell someone. Get it off his chest."

"But that's so weird that Ken and Lydia would be in the same campground as Frank Willis. Don't you think?" Julie asked.

"I think the chances of that happening are slim to none if you ask me," Stan said.

Rachel said, "Well, he said he told the police. Let's let them do what they do best. If he did do it, they'll find out."

"You're right, I know. But I just want this to be over," Stan said.

"We all do, Stan, but we're here for now, so we might as well make the best of it." So tell me, you said crappie was good eatin'. How good?"

"Ooh. It's almost sweet it's so good."

For the next three hours the group immersed themselves in conversation other than Frank Willis. Rachel learned that fishermen kept crappie hole locations a secret so they could catch a 'mess of 'em'. Julie told the group about their hike, the steep hills, cold refreshing water, and the two boobs at the base of a pine tree.

"Maybe you stumbled on to Mother Nature taking a nap," Stan joked.

The six night visitors of different backgrounds and religious beliefs talked about gun control, children and grandchildren, the war on terrorism and camping. Around midnight John and Rose said goodnight and wandered off to their camper. Stan and Lois followed shortly after, leaving Rachel and Julie to enjoy the dying embers of the fire and the soft night sky.

"That was nice," Julie sighed. "But I tell ya, I just can't get that guy running across the campground out of my head. I know he stashed something in the woods. Want to go look for it?"

Rachel gasped. "I know you've had some wine, but are you drunk? No way! I thought we agreed to let the police handle that."

"But they won't be back until tomorrow."

"So?"

"So what if whatever it was is important?"

"Julie, you need to let the police look for it. Not you."

Julie was silent for a few seconds, then stood up. "I'm gonna see what I can find."

Rachel shook her head. "You are so hard-headed. Just like your brother. You're gonna get us in trouble. But if you're going, I'll go with you. I think you're crazy, especially doing this at night. But let me get my flashlight. That way I can point you out to the paramedics."

Julie went inside the bus and returned with a flashlight and a set of walkie talkies.

"Here, if we lose sight of each other we can use these."

Rachel rolled her eyes in amazement. "I don't believe we're doing this. This is nuts."

"Oh, come on. It'll be fun. We'll pretend we're looking for that ten thousand bucks. If we find something, we'll call Matt."

"Well let's get going on this excellent adventure," Rachel huffed.

They marched through the moonless night toward the trail head.

"Okay. Now what?" Rachel asked, still miffed at her sister-in-law.

"Well, he was only gone ten minutes, so he couldn't have gone in very far. Why don't we split up? You take the area near the red trails. I'll go to the green trails. We'll look around for about ten minutes and then come back here. Then we'll both look down the yellow trails."

"Okay, but keep in touch."

It was pitch black; the going was slow.

"Anything yet?" Rachel called over the walkie talkie.

"Nope." Julie didn't know what she was looking for, just that it looked like something wrapped up in maybe a towel or a newspaper. She aimed her beam at the ground and into nearby bushes.

"Julie. I don't see anything. I'm moving over to the other trail," Rachel's voice squawked.

"Okay, Rach. I'm heading back to the yellow trails. I'll wait for you there."

Julie continued to search the ground while walking back toward the meeting place. When Rachel arrived, they split up again, each taking separate trails. The night was quiet except for the occasional hoot owl and the howls of distant coyotes. Julie stopped briefly to listen to the night sounds. *What a beautiful night. I guess everyone's right. I am a certifiable tree hugger. And I love it.*

In a brushy area she strained her eyes to see anything that looked like it might be a package. Nothing. Just an old, fallen limb. *Well, this really was a stupid idea. It's just too dark. Rachel's right. Matt can do this tomorrow.*

She turned around to make her way out of the brush. Suddenly the beam from her flashlight caught something in a nearby hollowed out tree. There it was; it looked like wad of newspapers. "Rachel, I think I found something. Come quick. I'll swing my flashlight around so you can find me."

"On my way, miss bionic eyes."

Julie bent down, reached into the tree and pulled out the package. She laid it on the ground and unwrapped it slowly. When she saw the contents, she shrank back in horror. Inside the wad of papers was a long, thin knife… and it was covered with blood.

Chapter 18

Alton Police Station
Alton, Missouri

Matt and Sarah compared notes on the short drive from Big Forest Campground to the Alton Police station. "So Atwater knew our vic, huh?"

"Yeah, and he made no bones about the fact that he was glad the guy was dead," Sarah said. "He says he had nothing to do with it, but I still need to talk to his wife to corroborate his alibi. What about yours?"

"A couple of interesting ones. One guy's a Vietnam vet and hates oddballs. You know, the kind that sneak around at night. He's got a temper, too. Then I've got the maintenance man. He was off bumpin' boots with some chickie and says he was with her until four in the morning. It sounds credible, but I gotta check his alibi and then get the T.O.D. And I didn't pick up on any animosity towards Willis. The others don't seem to have any reason to see the guy dead, either. I still can't dismiss that this was done by someone other than the people in the campground, though. You know...a random act of not-so-kindness."

"I hate to say this, but I hope it's one of our campers. Trying to track down a random killer won't be easy. Not in this area."

"Yeah, I know."

Matt's watch read five thirty five when Sarah turned the police cruiser into the parking lot and eased it into a space.

"All this stuff, the cell, the laptop, the vic's wallet, the beer can, the stuff from the hole...all of it's gonna have to go to the state police lab at Jefferson City," Sarah said.

"I know," Matt replied. "And that's a long drive. It'll take forever, and I don't want to wait forever. I'm gonna call Barry and see if he can help us out. He works the night shift a lot of times. Maybe I'll get lucky."

They walked into police headquarters at 101 Pine Street and headed straight for the War Room; it served many purposes – from meetings and interrogations to strategy sessions to birthday and retirement celebrations. Three large white chalk boards hugged the front wall of the War Room; several conference tables were strewn about in the center. A telephone nestled on a small table in the corner next to the chalk boards, while two metal folding chairs leaned lazily against the wall by the door. A large map of Missouri hung on one wall.

Matt grabbed the phone and pulled out his pocket directory. He dialed the number of the Jefferson City State Police Crime Lab.

Sergeant Barry Pritchard was surprised to hear Matt's voice this late at night. "What's up, Matt? Been to any more latent fingerprint classes lately?"

"No, but that one sure was fun, wasn't it?"

"Yeah it was. Don't tell me...you're calling to collect on your bet."

"Now Barry, would I do that to you?"

"Why not? I'd do it to you. What do you need?"

"Help on a rush job."

"What have you got?"

"I need to get an evidence box to your forensics lab ASAP. I have a homicide on my hands at a local campground and I don't want to lose any of my suspects."

"You and everybody else. Where are you now?"

"I'm at my station down here in Alton, but the homicide was at Big Forest Campground. I don't need everything done right away. But what I DO need is a laptop and a cell processed tonight."

"Big Forest, huh? That's a nice place. The wife and I have been there several times. You must be livin' right, buddy. Things have been pretty slow here this week. Let me see what I can do. I'll call you back in about ten minutes."

"I'll be here," Matt said and gave Barry the Alton station's phone number. While he waited, he opened a chair and eased one of the tables up next to the white boards. Sarah found a dry crasc marker and began to detail the murder and the possible suspects.

On one white board she wrote the victim's name, *Frank Willis – AKA Arthur Hatcher*. She had just finished noting the details of Frank's life and death, when Matt's cell phone rang. It was the pathologist, Theresa Dawson.

"Sorry I couldn't be there for the unveiling, doc," Matt said.

"Not a problem. But you know, I thought I was done with this stuff when I retired and left St. Louis for the simple life, but apparently you're determined to help me keep my skills up to date."

"Sorry, doc. Not my doing."

"Anyway, not to worry, I got pictures for you, and a good set of prints for comparison."

"Well, what's the word?"

"My preliminary findings are that C.O.D was exsanguination. At first I thought your victim was shot, but when I looked closer, I determined he took a single stab wound to the belly. He didn't have much fat up front to help him out. The trajectory of the entry wound indicates a straight-forward thrust, so the victim was facing his killer when he was stabbed. As luck would have it, the weapon severed the abdominal aortic artery. He would have bled out pretty fast. I saw from the pictures you took…by the way, you have a knack with that camera."

"What can I say? It's a gift."

"Yeah, right. Apparently he was found floating in a pool. I checked his lungs, but they were clear, so he didn't drown."

Matt jotted the data on the white board. "What about the weapon?"

"The blade was long, I'd say eight inches, and pretty thin. I didn't find any other visible wounds or trauma on the body. No defensive wounds to the hands. Nothing under the nails, either. I'd say he was taken by surprise and had no time to put up a fight. The only personal effect on the body was a small piece of gold paper with an eight digit number typed on it. It was in his right front pocket."

"What about T.O.D? He was found floating in the pool at about 6:00 a.m."

"Time of death is somewhere between one-thirty and three-thirty a.m. Anybody here to ID the body?"

"No, not yet. We think he's a widower. We've got his personal phone book and his cell and computer. Hopefully we'll find something. Thanks, doc. I guess you'll have to keep him on ice for now. I'll get back to you about next of kin. And thanks for working late. I owe you."

"Hey, next time you're on your way over, stop at the Sweetheart Bakery and pick me up a cup of coffee and a cinnamon roll."

"Will do."

Matt turned his attention back to the white board, added the date, cause and time of death. On the next line he wrote, *Willis was from New Jersey. His original name was Hatcher.*

He pulled over the next white board and wrote the names of the office staff, campers and any notes from the interviews he and Sarah conducted:

Phil, Donna, Eric O'Neal
No motive at this time
Barely knew victim
Eric heard digging sound outside

John and Rose Maynard
Cattle farmers
Hate crime?

Stan and Lois Yates
Daughter murdered 10 yrs ago
   Motive?
   Willis is from Jersey

Hal and Harriet Evans
Mr. Security
Mr. has issues with door
handles

Tom and Carolyn Pettyjohn
Vietnam vet with
combat experience
Doesn't like sneaky people
Gets mad easily

Jerry and Trina Hancock
check geotreasures for
 winner of $

Howard Kraft and Sheila Young
Check Ryan for alibi
Works at True Value – nights

Julie saw unidentified sub
 running to trailhead with
 package and returning
 without it – Search woods

Ken and Lydia Atwater
Shaky alibi – knew vic
Interview wife

Sonny Wallace
check Mississippi addr
check alibi – 4 a.m.

He stepped back from the boards and looked at the scribbles. "Well, what's the connection?"

Sarah read her notes. "I don't know. I can't see it. No one except Ken Atwater had a motive. And he was honest about knowing, and hating, Frank Willis. I still need to talk to his wife, though."

"But it doesn't make sense. Why would Atwater admit that he knew Frank?" Matt asked.

"Maybe to divert suspicion to someone else," Sarah said. "Or maybe just being honest."

"Well, maybe we need to consider someone from outside the campground," Matt said. "It's a remote area and anyone could drive or walk in there." He opted to keep that scenario for last. "Let's see what's in the billfold."

He went to his desk and found a pair of latex gloves, slipped them on and opened Frank's billfold searching for any clues. Inside was a Missouri driver's license, a VISA credit card and a social security card. No money, just a receipt from the local True Value for a roll of duct tape. It was dated two days ago. Matt looked back at the white boards.

"True Value? Somebody works at the True Value. Howard Kraft works there. I need to verify his alibi," he muttered. He picked up the phone and dialed Ryan Ashmore's number. Minutes later, he hung up and noted the white board that Kraft's alibi was solid.

Sarah stood to leave the room. "Need anything from me?"

"Yeah," Matt replied. He handed her a list of the camper names. "Can you check to see if any of these have a record, and if anyone has been in New Jersey in the last two years?"

"Sure. No problem. I haven't had supper yet. Pizza & More sound good? Looks like it might be a long night."

"Thanks, that works for me. Extra pepperoni," he said and checked his notebook for a certain Donaphan phone number. It was time to discreetly confirm where Sonny spent his evening.

The young woman in Donaphan said Sonny was with her until around four a.m, then left for his camper. She spoke softly - an indication that the husband – or the boyfriend – was nearby. Matt assured her that her secret was safe with him, and noted the chalk board with the information.

Sounds like Sonny was telling me the truth. I'm startin' to think he doesn't look good for this murder. No bells or sirens goin' off...at least not yet. He would not omit the maintenance man entirely, but his level of interest in Buford Lee Wallace had just plunged dramatically. He decided to look elsewhere.

Chapter 19

State Police Crime Lab
Jefferson City, Missouri

Sergeant Pritchard picked up his phone and called down to Kyle Danner, one of several Computer Evidence Recovery Specialists who worked at the Missouri State Police Crime lab in Jefferson City.

"Hey Kyle, I know your shift is just about over, but can you work late for a rush job? It's for Matt Baker. He's got a dead body on his hands and a computer and cell phone that need to be processed."

There was no hesitation in Kyle's voice. "Sure. No problem. Is the evidence box here now?"

"No, it should be here sometime around eight o'clock."

"I'll grab a quick bite and work on some other stuff till you call me." Kyle loved his job, and was considered a true "geek" by his coworkers. He relished the thrill of the cyber hunt, as well as the adrenaline rush he got when he found valuable evidence. If it came down to work or home, everyone knew where Kyle would rather be.

Sergeant Pritchard called Matt with the news. "Get somebody on the road with that stuff. We've got a tech who's willing to work on it for you. His name's Kyle Danner."

"Thanks, Barry. Now I owe you."

"I know. And believe me, I'll collect," he laughed. "I'll have Kyle call you when your stuff arrives."

The Alton patrol car left the parking lot on a marathon run to Jefferson City with its lights flashing. Three hours later it pulled into the parking lot of the State Police Crime Lab. The officer made his way to the third floor where he handed the evidence box over to Sergeant Pritchard, who promptly recorded receipt of it, and then picked up his phone and called Kyle.

Matt munched on his pizza and looked at his notes, revisiting each interview he and Sarah conducted that day. He was trying to come up with the smallest hint of a motive. It still kept coming back to Ken Atwater. He had motive, and he had opportunity. But did he have means? No weapon had been found. *Definitely have to look in the woods tomorrow.*

Around midnight, Sarah stepped into the War Room. "Can't find any records on any of these names. Any progress on your end?"

"No, I still can't come up with what I think is a good motive. But I can't rule out someone from outside the campground. Let's hope Jeff City has some luck."

Just then the phone rang.

"Detective Baker."

"Detective, it's Kyle from the crime lab."

"Hey, Kyle. Thanks for working this for me."

"No prob. First off, the cell phone. That one was easy. It has nothing on it. No calls out, no calls in. Your vic must have kept it just for emergencies."

Matt noted the chalk board with cell phone information. "Okay, got it."

"So now I've got the computer here in front of me. I'll call you as soon as I'm finished."

"This is a real rush job, Kyle. I'll wait to hear from you."

"I'm workin' on it as we speak." Kyle hung up, turned on the laptop, and began his search. He would use special software, known as a write blocker. The software was designed to protect the evidentiary integrity of any data Kyle might find. "Okay little buddy. Let's talk. You know I'm in a hurry, so spit it out. No need for a complete copy right now. Just cough up a preview for me. Then we'll give it to our buddy, Matt," he said looking at the last access dates.

Thirty minutes later Kyle was calling Matt again. "I found some history files of Internet use. I can fax you the screen images if that will help."

"Great," Matt replied. He gave Kyle the fax number and waited. Within a few seconds the fax machine whined to life and belched out several pages.

"I hope you found something good, Kyle," Matt said. His eyes poured over the pages looking for something that would point him to a murderer.

"Hello. What have we here?" The first sheet detailed Frank's recent access to a site named geotreasures.com. Another sheet showed that Frank had searched and found several GPS coordinates. The last sheet listed chat logs on the geotreasures website. *Geotreasures. That's familiar.* Matt thought. He glanced up at the chalkboard. There it was. Trina and Jerry Hancock...*geotreasures.com.* He rushed to the phone and called Kyle.

"Well, any help?" Kyle asked.

"I think so, but I need to get a subpoena for the IP address on that chat log."

"How soon do you need it?"

"Uh...yesterday!"

"It just so happens this is your lucky yesterday. I've got a contact in the legal department who is available to us 24/7. I'll call her right now."

"Great."

The wait was agonizing. "Come on. Come on, man," he pleaded as he glared at the phone. The extra pepperoni was beginning to talk back to him.

What seemed like an eternity was actually only twenty minutes, and Matt grabbed the phone on the first ring. He could hear the excitement in Kyle's voice. "Got your subpoena, Matt. I'll contact the service provider and get your address. Give me half an hour."

"Kyle, you da man!"

Twenty five minutes later Kyle was giving Matt the name for the chat log. "The name's Jerry Hancock. Know him?"

"I certainly do! Kyle, I owe you big time, buddy.

"Just doin' my job."

Matt hung up the phone. "Sarah. Let's go. We need to get back to the campground. Now!"

Chapter 20

Big Forest Campground

"Hello, Julie." The voice came from behind.

Julie whirled around to see a dark, hooded figure standing about six feet away. Her heart raced and sweat streamed down her back; her breath came in rapid spurts. She squinted and shined her flashlight in the direction of the voice. The figure stepped closer and removed the hood from their sweatshirt. Julie breathed a sigh of relief.

"Oh, hi. It's…Trina, right?" she said. "Wow, you scared me."

"Sorry about that," Trina said coldly. "I was just taking a late night stroll when I heard a sound coming from over here." Trina seemed to be staring right through Julie.

Julie stood in front of the knife and tried to act casual. "Funny, I couldn't sleep either," she said. "Fresh air sounded good. I guess I had too much wine, you know…headache. I thought a walk would help." Her legs shook, but nervous energy kept her talking. "I felt like I was going to throw up, so I just came over here. I'm better now, so I'll just leave you to your walk. Nice talking to you. See you later," she said and began to walk back toward the path.

"I can't let you do that," Trina whispered stepping in front of her.

"What do you mean?" Julie gasped, wide eyed.

"You found it, didn't you?" Trina stepped closer.

"Found what?"

"The knife. You found it."

"I don't know what…"

"I can't let anyone else see it, Julie."

Julie steeled herself against the panic. *Maybe if I can keep her talking, Rachel will hear us and get over here to help.* "So," she said, stepping aside and nodding towards the opened newspaper. "Is that what killed Frank Willis?" she asked loudly.

Trina stopped and stared at the long, blood-soaked blade. She dropped all pretense now. "You don't understand," she said. "He won all the time. He took prizes out of our hands so many times. It's not fair. I wasn't going to let it happen to us again. Not this time!" She clenched her fists; her body shook with rage.

Julie was confused. "What are you talking about?"

"He plays the geo game too," Trina said coldly. "The skinny little bastard sits up there in that junk heap of his and gets all the clues as soon as they're posted. Then he goes out at night and finds them before anyone else. That's how he wins, he cheats! Well, not this time." Foam seeped from the corners of her mouth and her eyes narrowed.

"How do you know he plays the game? Don't you use code names on the website?"

"I'm pretty good with tracking things," Trina said. "It's easy if you know what you're doing."

Trina's voice reduced to barely a whisper. "So I knew it was him. That he was ITISMINE. I followed him last night, after Jerry went to sleep. I knew he was headed for the final coordinate, and he'd get the last clue. I figured, why should I get my hands dirty? Let him do all the work. It was in a box buried next to the light pole out front." Her face contorted as she described the scene. "He was so proud of himself. Prancing around like Rocky Balboa. So, when he got to the parking lot, I stopped him and told him he wasn't gonna take this prize from us. He laughed in my face! But he stopped laughing when I reminded him about Todd Dillon."

"Who?"

"Todd, the geo treasure hunter who died in Cleveland a while back. What a shame," she said and shook her head. "But you know he shouldn't have been standing so close to that ridge." Trina's eyes glazed over and she giggled when she remembered the horror on Todd's face when he fell to his death.

Julie was terrified now. *This woman's crazy!* "You...saw him die? But you didn't kill him, did you?"

Trina shot back. "You're a bright girl. You figure it out."

Julie's eyes grew wide. "You killed him."

"Not exactly. It was an accident. We were both trying to get to the spot where the clue was. He pushed me first, and I pushed back. Oops." She covered her mouth with her hand.

"Even if it was an accident, you still killed him."

"But I got the prize." Trina flashed a wicked grin.

"Then you killed Frank Willis just to get the grand prize?"

"The *ten* grand prize. You are a bright girl, aren't you?" Trina said sarcastically. "You should have seen him. It was priceless. I wish I'd had a camera. The little weasel didn't think I had the guts." She cocked her head slightly. "Well, you know what they say? It gets easier the more times you do it. Problem is he ran before I could get the clue out of his greasy little pocket. I guess nobody's gonna win this time. Maybe they'll roll it over and the next prize will be more. That would be fun."

"But it's just a game."

Trina's eyes narrowed. "I don't play games when it comes to money."

"Money?"

"Yeah, you know. The stuff that makes the world go round," Trina said and turned around in mock dance. "You ought to try it sometime. It's exhilarating."

"There's not enough money in the world," Julie said.

"There is when you don't have any. I used to have money. Jerry and I both did. We took vacations, had nice cars, the works. But we both lost our jobs. Ended up tracking down stolen cars for minimum wage."

"But it's honest work." Julie said.

"You don't understand. It was okay with Jerry, but I couldn't stand it. I guess I'm just greedy. Then we fell into this treasure hunt thing. We won a few trips and that helped for a while. But when the ten grand showed up, I knew I had to have it. It would be the first step to digging ourselves out of that minimum wage hole.

Julie was stalling now, hoping that Rachel was on her way. She looked down at the bloodstained blade. "This is your knife?"

"No. It was in the bottom of a fishing boat. I figured it wouldn't be missed, so I just took it." Trina's eyes shifted back to the knife. "I stashed it in the tree trunk last night and was on my way to bury it. I'm really sorry you found it. So, you see," she whispered. "I can't let you tell anyone. You know too much now."

Julie's legs trembled. "Trina, you're sick and need help. You need to turn yourself into the police."

"You're not as bright as I thought," Trina chuckled. "Don't you know? There's a killer running around out here. Why, someone going out late at night, especially out here in the dark…they're just asking for trouble."

She paused and sighed deeply, then lifted up a large shovel. "Oh, and by the way, I don't think your friend will be helping you." The blade was covered with dark hair and blood.

Julie froze. "No! Rachel!" she gasped.

"It seems the murderer will collect two more victims tonight."

Trina took another step forward and reached down for the knife. Julie shifted her weight and kicked up with her right foot directly into Trina's jaw. It was a direct hit; Trina fell to the ground, dazed and moaning.

Julie stood paralyzed for a moment, her brain trying to process what had just happened. She did the first thing that popped into her mind - she sprinted away, into the darkness. She stopped briefly to look over her shoulder only to see Trina stumble to her feet and lurch after her. She had to get away somehow. The campground was too far away for anyone to hear her call for help. Her instincts took over and she did the only thing she could do – she ran into the wilderness.

Chapter 21

July, 1870
Oregon County Missouri

Victoria hung the raccoon pelt over the maple tree branch. It had been a good day, five pelts skinned and drying. She washed her knife in the nearby stream, turned and walked toward the two gravesites nearby.

"Well, Papa, Uncle is taking me to Pilot Knob tomorrow to sell the pelts. People are coming from a place called New York to buy them. Uncle says they take the best ones and make coats and hats with them and sell them to the rich people. He tells me I'll get a lot of money for my skins. He says I'm the best skinner he's ever seen. I told him I was taught by the best. I won't stay long. I promise."

In the six years since the trial and execution of Skunk Adams, the Civil War had ended, the nation survived, and Victoria had made a life for herself in the tiny cabin on the hill. She continued to trap and make furs, but recently felt that something was missing. Even though her aunt and uncle were close by, she was lonely. After all, she had been on her own since she was twelve.

She adjusted the small, white rocks that marked her mother's grave. "Remember when I told you about the town near the fort? It's called Pilot Knob. Uncle and I left for home after the soldiers put Skunk Adams in the ground and we didn't go into the town. Well, I finally get to go there and sell my pelts. Oh,

Mama, I'm excited to go, but very glad Uncle will be there with me."

According to Francois' instructions, she had packed provisions for two nights, rolled them in her blanket and placed it near the front door. Francois said they would leave early in the morning, and she wanted to be ready.

The sun had barely peeked up over the horizon when Francois knocked on her door. "Are you awake, *mon doux*?"

"*Oui*, Uncle," she replied. She stepped out onto the porch, shivering with excitement. "Will there be many people there?"

"I don't know, but the last time I went, there were many. You will enjoy it. I cannot wait to see the look on their faces when they learn some of these pelts to be yours."

The journey would not be an easy one; the trail would take them through thick, overgrown forest. But Victoria would have walked through fire to get to Pilot Knob.

"Uncle, what's a city like?" she asked, stepping over a fallen log.

"Oh, let me tell you, it is a big place. Many people live there. Women in pretty dresses and big wide hats, and men pushing and shoving to go somewhere, where I do not know. They are in such a rush. And it is very noisy."

"Noisy?"

"*Oui*. Sounds...like people talking and laughing. Horses stomping in the street. Wagons going bump, bump. You will see."

They kept a steady pace, Francois was anxious to get there, too, but for different reasons than Victoria. "I do not care much for city life," he said. "There are just too many people. I have grown old on the mountain and I like it that way. But the money and goods are in the city. Two times a year is enough."

"How long will we be at Pilot Knob?" she asked.

"We will be there for two days. Then home."

Victoria said, anxiously. "Two days? What do we do for two days?"

"We talk to other fur traders, to buyers. We look at their furs and they look at ours. We trade them for supplies or sell them for money. We will eat at a fine restaurant. Then we will buy what we need and come back. Do not look at me that way. I will not let any harm come to you."

She dreamed about the city each night on the trail. Of fair skinned women dressed in bright red and blue dresses and feathered hats, strutting arm in arm with handsome men in dark blue pants and coats; of gnarly-faced, toothless trappers trying to pull her pelts away from her without paying for them; of being lost in a sea of people and calling for her uncle and not finding him; of being rescued by a smiling young man who asked what her name was and she couldn't speak so he left her alone. *I'll be glad to get to this city so my mind can calm down.*

They saw the dust rising over the tops of the trees from a mile away. "There it is. That is Pilot Knob, *mon doux*." The pelts, once a heavy burden strapped across her back, seemed weightless now. She held his hand as they walked down Main Street, stepping up on to the wooden sidewalk to avoid all the horse traffic.

"What do we do now?" she asked wide-eyed. Her head swiveled from side to side, trying to see everything.

"We find the place where the traders are. And then we trade and sell."

They stopped an elderly gentleman and asked if he knew
where the fur traders were. He directed them to turn left at the
bank building. "You'll see the stables. That's where you want
to be."

Victoria was amazed. She covered her ears to block the noise
of horses snorting, their hooves stomping the hard earth as they
pulled wagons and buckboards, and of people shouting, trying to
be heard over the din of the bustling crowd.

Francois had to pull her along; she was too busy looking at the
buildings and the people to watch where she was going.

At each storefront she stopped briefly to see what mysteries
lie inside. Francois understood. *Let the girl see it all.* He
stopped at the front door of Henry's General Store.

"Do you want to go in?" he asked.

"Yes. You'll go in too, won't you?"

"*Oui,*" he said and led her inside.

The short, balding storekeeper in a neat, white apron came out
from behind the counter. "Good morning, sir and miss. Is there
anything I can help you find today?

"Good morning. My niece, it is her first time here. She wants
to look."

"Oh, please do, miss. Is this your first time in Pilot Knob?"

"It's my first time in a city," Victoria said.

His eyes widened with delight. "Well, welcome to both of
you, then. Please, take your time. Can I show you something?"
He spied her furs. "My, those are some beautiful pelts you have.
That raccoon is especially nice. Are you selling them?"

"Yes, but if you like it, you may have it."

"Oh, goodness no. I...I couldn't do that. But....I could trade
you for it. I tell you what, if you see anything in the store, I'll
trade it to you for that fur. How does that sound?"

Victoria looked at Francois. He winked and nodded.

"That will be fine, but I don't know what I want."

"Just take your time. Perhaps some flour or sugar. Or perhaps some cloth or buttons to make a nice skirt. Or perhaps something for your sweet tooth?"

Victoria smiled at the clerk. "Perhaps."

"If you don't know what you like, you can return later. Is it a deal?"

"It's a deal." She handed the pelt to the clerk who placed it behind the counter.

"I'd like to return later today."

"I'll be here."

Several traders had already camped behind the stables. Francois led Victoria to a vacant area near the corral. Everyone stared at them, word had spread that a woman trapper would be there and that her pelts were the finest.

"Well, let's have a gander at them there skins little lady," one grizzled trapper snarled. Victoria hesitated, remembering her dream, but laid her pelts on the ground for all to see. The men gathered around and fondled the furs. Some nodded approval while others walked slump-shouldered back to their cache.

"I tell you, the others, they liked them," Francois beamed.

Victoria smiled and hugged him.

The fur buyers arrived later that afternoon and Victoria's pelts sold quickly; she made a lot of money and was reassured that her talent was worth it. The afternoon dragged on, and she grew bored waiting for Francois to finish.

"Uncle, I'm going to go back to the store and make my choice."

"Be careful, *mon doux*. I will wait for you here."

Her step was lighter now, not just because the pelts that weighed her down were gone, but because she was proud of what she had just done. She had out-skint the skinners.

When she entered the store, the clerk called out to her. "You've returned!"

"Yes, and I've decided to take the buttons, if that's alright with you."

"Of course it is."

He reached under the counter and pulled out a small bag containing various sized buttons and placed it on the counter. "There you are, miss. Oh, and before you leave I want you to meet someone. Mr. Yochem, this is the young lady I was telling you about. The one who gave me the raccoon fur you liked so much."

A man standing near a shelf of canned fruit turned and walked toward Victoria. He doffed his hat. "How do you do? My name is Rogers Yochem, but most folks around here just call me Dutch. Mr. Henry showed me the fur you gave him. It's very beautiful. Might I inquire if you have others for sale?"

Victoria stared back. *He's so handsome. What do I say? His eyes, they're so deep and blue. His smile...* Her cheeks flushed.

"Do you have any still for sale?" he repeated.

"Oh. No. I mean..." *Silly girl. Speak to the man. He'll leave if you don't speak.*

"I...I sold them all to the fur buyers."

He sensed her anxiety. "You are not here alone are you? Are you here with someone?

"No...I mean yes, I came with my uncle."

"Where did you learn your trade? From your uncle?"

"No, my papa taught me." Her throat was dry. "My parents are both dead. My uncle brought me here to sell my furs." She looked at him. *He's not going away.*

"Well, they must have been very pretty." He hesitated. "Forgive me for being so forward as I don't even know you. But...you have the most beautiful eyes."

Chapter 22

Big Forest Campground

Julie barreled into the black night. She could hear Trina gasping for breath close behind. She tripped over an outcropping of rocks and fell, tearing a large gash in her knee. Her flashlight crashed to the ground and shattered. *No!* She scrambled to her feet and raced down the sloping path, grasping tree branches and feeling for bushes and tree trunks. Groping in the darkness, she could hear Trina calling to her.

"Hey, Julie, guess what I got? You left the knife."

Crap! *Go! Go!* She tried to run quietly, but leaves and twigs crunched under her feet and kept giving her position away.

The thorn bushes were unforgiving, tearing at her clothes and ripping the flesh on her face, arms and legs. Fueled by a rush of adrenaline, Julie flailed through the briars as fast as her aching legs would carry her. Her lungs burned, but she knew she had to keep moving.

She groped deeper into the dark, dank forest, hoping to shake her pursuer. She ran for what seemed like an eternity, and then slowed to a walk hoping to catch her breath. She bent forward, gasping. The air was moist and musty – almost suffocating. Her arm pressed against a large tree, its rough bark scraped her skin. She quickly leaped behind the massive trunk and leaned against it for support. *I need to rest. Just for a second.* She whispered softly. "Somebody help me. Michael…Victoria, I wish one of you was here."

Suddenly she heard Trina roar. "I'll get you, you bitch! I'll kill you!"

She froze. The voice was close now. So close the hair on the back of her neck stood up. Then, the forest was deathly silent. Julie's heightened senses couldn't detect any sound or movement. She stood motionless, her heart exploding in her chest. Her brain screamed again - m*ove! Now!*

Before she could take another step, she felt a hand grab her right wrist tightly. She wanted to scream but couldn't. She turned to face her attacker only to see the dim likeness of a slender, dark woman pursing her lips with her index finger, a signal to remain quiet. Julie held her breath.

Both women stood for a few moments. Then the woman tugged on Julie's arm, beaconing her to follow. Julie couldn't move her feet. *Who is this? Where did she come from?* The woman tugged on her arm again...this time harder. Julie didn't think; she just followed – away from Trina. They ran through the dark, over fallen logs and around bushes. Julie was numb, blindly following the shadow that gripped her arm.

Julie soon realized that she wasn't being torn by briars or tripping over rocks or roots, and she wasn't gasping for air. What was happening? She was running, but as if on a cloud. The woman eventually slowed to a walk and Julie fell in behind her. They finally emerged from a mass of brush and trees onto a narrow path. Julie knew they were near a stream; she could hear water rippling and felt the cool, moist air on her face.

It was then that the woman stopped. To their right stood a small cabin, soft light pouring through the front window welcomed them and shown softly on two small piles of white stones nearby. Julie's eyes grew wide as she surveyed the scene. *Where am I? Someone lives here?*

The woman turned to Julie and said, "Come inside. You will be safe here. Come." She smiled and gently pulled Julie toward the porch steps.

Weary from her ordeal, Julie slowly stepped onto the porch and into the tiny cabin. She squinted at first, the light from the fireplace, though soft and dim, hurt her eyes. After a few seconds, she was able to see more clearly and look around. The cabin was small, but clean; a single table, adorned with an oil lantern, stood near the stone fireplace. Snuggled against the far wall was a small cot covered with some kind of large animal skin. A table with gnarled tree limbs for legs stood against the opposite wall, a large bowl and pitcher sat atop. Next to the fireplace lay a small pyramid of dry wood. Julie felt a sense of warmth and love. It was as if she had walked into her own house.

The woman spoke. "Please, sit down, you must be tired."

She was slightly taller than Julie and thin, with dark skin the color of aged copper, and pale golden eyes. Julie guessed her age at somewhere around eighty years. Her black hair, laced with strands of gray was set in a long braid that drifted gracefully down her back. She wore a long dark blue cotton skirt and a red and white plaid blouse. Julie sat down heavily and sighed, thankful to feel safe.

"I'll get you some water. Are you hungry?" the woman asked.

"Thank you, I'll take the water, but I'm not hungry," Julie said.

The woman stepped toward the front door and grabbed the handle of a large bucket sitting nearby. "I won't be long," she said and closed the door behind her. A few moments later she returned. She dipped a large wooden ladle into the bucket and offered it to Julie, who drank thirstily; the water was cool and refreshing.

The old woman looked at Julie's bleeding knee. "Let me put something on that," she said and walked to a small wooden box near the fireplace. She pulled a large, leather bag from the box and motioned Julie to put her leg out. The woman dipped a cloth into the bucket of water and wiped the blood from Julie's knee. She then quickly put a generous amount of dark blue powder on the wound. The bleeding stopped immediately, and Julie felt the pain subside. The woman then sat across the table and looked at Julie with loving eyes.

Eventually her thirst was quenched, and Julie peered at the woman. "Who are you?" she asked.

"You've been looking for me, Julie," the old woman replied.

"How do you know my name?" Julie gasped.

"I've always known your name, Julie. I'm your great-grandmother. I'm Victoria."

Julie sat motionless, stunned. "I...I don't understand. That's impossible. You...you died before I was born."

Victoria said softly. "I've been near you, my dear, you just didn't know it. Whenever you speak my name, I draw near. You began to search for me a long time ago, and I've stayed close to you since then, watching you all along. I couldn't let that woman hurt you. I had to do something. So, I brought you to my home, to safety."

"But, this is crazy!"

"The spirits of our ancestors are always near, Julie. And spirits are not ruled by the living world."

"Spirits?" Julie shook her head in disbelief.

"My ancestors...your ancestors are of the Cherokee tribe, the Deer Clan. We all die, Julie, but our spirits remain, in the Spirit World."

"But this cabin, you live in this cabin? In the Spirit World?"

"My papa owned this land many years ago. He and my mama built this cabin. I was born here."

"This is insane. I must be dreaming."

"Anything is possible, my dear. You must believe," Victoria said and held her hands out toward Julie. Julie looked into Victoria's eyes, then slowly, with slight trepidation, reached out and took the old woman's hands. She immediately felt a surge of energy pulse through her body; she tightened her grip on the gnarly fingers. The old woman smiled, and Julie knew then that she was looking at the face of her great-grandmother. She was touching Victoria.

"Listen to me, my child. Listen to the stories I'm going to tell you. And remember them so you can tell your children and they can tell their children."

They sat at the small table in the tiny cabin and Victoria told Julie her story. She explained how she got the name Eagle Eyes. "The Cherokee people always wanted to have peace with the white man so we adopted many of their ways. We have two names - one is Cherokee, the other is English. While my English name is in honor of Queen Victoria, my Cherokee name is for the color of my eyes."

Victoria shared her grief and told how Amy died and Henri was killed and of almost losing her life to Skunk Adams that winter evening. "My mother was watching me from the Spirit World. I knew I was going to die, so I called out to her. She came to me in a field. I ran to her and we hugged. She folded her arms around me and made both of us invisible and Skunk Adams ran right past us. Mama and I spent the night talking about things she wanted to tell me before she died. She told me that she was always with me, watching over me, that when I spoke her name she would be nearby."

"What are the two piles of rocks outside your door?" Julie asked.

"Those mark my mama and papa's graves. Mama's is nearest the porch," Victoria replied softly. "Let me show you something." She reached inside the neck of her blouse and pulled out her father's good luck charm. "This was my papa's. He wore it to keep him safe while hunting in the forest. Would you like to hold it?"

"Yes, I would," Julie replied. Victoria removed the necklace and handed it to Julie who gently cradled the cougar claw. Speechless and tearful, she closed her hand around the charm; the sharp claw dug into her palm.

Victoria told how she learned about medicine from her Aunt Catey. "My aunt was from the Blue Clan. She was a strong medicine woman who taught me how to use the plants in the forest to heal. And she showed me the power of the blue powder. It can heal many things, including your knee." Julie looked down at her knee and shook her head in disbelief.

"But, how did you get to Graniteville?" Julie asked. "That's a long way from here."

Victoria shared her first visit to Pilot Knob. "His name was Rogers Yochem and he was a farmer. But everyone called him Dutch. He was so handsome, and the first time I met him he told me I had beautiful eyes. He invited Uncle and me to his farm to stay with him. It was near Graniteville. Uncle said it was nice of him to offer and that we would go with him. We stayed two days, but Dutch wanted to see me again. And I him.

"Did you stay?"

"Yes, Uncle went back to the mountain, but I used some of the money I made selling my furs and took a room at the hotel in Pilot Knob. I stayed for many days and got to know this gentle man. When I told him I had to return to the mountain, he escorted me home. Then he asked Uncle for my hand."

Julie's jaw dropped. "What did he say?"

"It wasn't for my uncle to give permission. I told Uncle that Dutch was a good, honest man and that I wanted to marry him. I'm a Cherokee woman. Cherokee women have the power to chose who they want to be with. Dutch and I went back to Graniteville and married a month later. It was then that I moved to his farm. We made crops and made a family. First came Alfred, then your grandfather, Robert. After that it was Portia and Jesse."

"I found some letters from you to Dutch when I was cleaning out my mother's closet," Julie said.

Victoria leaned back in her chair. "Letters? What kind of letters?"

Julie smiled. "Oh, I remember that one of them said something like...I slept so soundly in your arms. That kind of stuff."

Victoria's brow wrinkled in thought, and then she clasped her hands to her chest. "Yes, I remember. We wrote little notes to each other all the time. He was so gentle and kind. I never fell out of love with him. But even love couldn't keep him here. He died in 1897. I decided to stay at the farm, but in 1936 it was my time to go to the Spirit World."

Victoria paused for a moment. "That's when I knew my mother was right. You see, when a Cherokee dies, we believe our souls go to the Spirit World. But they don't have to remain there for all eternity. We believe that our souls can move between the Spirit World and the living world. Most people can't see us. But you, you are special, Julie. Cherokee blood runs strong in your veins." She leaned forward and cradled

Julie's face in her hands. "My mama came from the Spirit World to save me and I knew that I could do the same for you."

Victoria sat straight in her chair and squared her shoulders. "You're also very brave and have great vision, like the eagle." She hesitated; her eagle eyes softened. "So you want to find where my body is buried?"

Julie nodded.

"Then go to the old Linkford Cemetery over by Graniteville. That's where you'll find our markers, Dutch's and mine. They're next to the twin oak trees." The room was still except for the soft crackle of the fire.

"Remember what I've told you Julie. It's your heritage. My blood…Cherokee blood, runs in your veins."

Julie gazed into the soft, golden eagle eyes of her great-grandmother. "I'll remember. I'm not sure my family will believe me, but I know it's true."

Victoria could see the events of the night were taking its toll on her great-granddaughter. Julie appeared to be exhausted. "You are tired, my dear. Go over and lie down on my bed. I'll wake you when it's morning."

"I'll be alright, grandmother," Julie said.

Victoria persisted. "Please, get some rest. I promise, you'll be safe here," she said and led Julie over to the bed. Julie let out a contented sigh as she snuggled down into the soft cougar skin pelt.

"Maybe just for a little while," she mumbled.

"Julie! Are you okay? Wake up, Julie."

She opened her eyes to find Matt shaking her. Suddenly she remembered all about the previous night and shot awake.

"Matt. I'm awake. You don't have to shake so hard."

"Oh, God, sis," he said with tears in his eyes. "You sure are." He hugged her so tight she thought her ribs would break.

"Are you okay?" he asked.

"I'm fine. Just a few scratches. Matt, it was Trina. She killed Frank Willis."

"We know. Are you sure you're alright?" he asked and hugged her again.

"I'm alright! But she's here, in the forest. She tried to kill me."

"It's okay. We found her earlier. She must have tripped on a rock. She was unconscious."

"Matt, Rachel was with me and Trina said she killed her."

"Rachel has a nasty bump on her head, but she'll be fine."

Julie wept with joy. "But, how did you know Trina killed Frank?"

"His computer told us. I'll fill you in when we get you back to the campground."

"Then how did you find me?"

"Good ole hiker finder."

Julie stuck her hand into her front pocket. There it was - the hiker finder. She forgot to take it out and turn it off after yesterday's hike. It had been on all this time. She hugged her brother and cried.

She stepped back and glanced around. "Where's the cabin?"

"What cabin?"

"Victoria's. See those two piles of stones? Those are the markers of her parents, our great-great-grandparents, Matt. Her cabin was right here."

Matt looked deeply into his sister's eyes, looking for signs of a concussion. "We'll check that out that later. Come on, let's go, sis."

He turned and looked at the other officers. "Somebody call Mike and tell him we've found her and she's fine. Tell him he can take his foot off the gas." They walked arm in arm up the trail toward the campground.

Julie looked at her brother, "Matt, Trina killed that other geo treasure hunt guy, Todd Dillon."

"What?"

"Yeah, she told me it was an accident. That he pushed her first and she pushed back and sent him off the cliff."

"Hey, two for the price of one. I'll get hold of Cleveland as soon as I get you back."

Julie continued. "Matt, don't think I'm crazy, but I met Victoria."

"Who?"

"Victoria, our great-grandmother. She saved me from Trina. She took me to her cabin. It was right back there. She put medicine on my knee."

Matt looked at his sister's knee and saw the remnants of a dark blue powder. "What are you saying, sis. You met our great-grandmother? She's dead."

"I know, I don't understand it either, but it's true. She came from the Spirit World and found me in the forest and took me to her cabin."

"Julie, that's impossible. Spirit World? You were out there all night. Are you sure you didn't fall and hit your head?"

"I didn't Matt. I'm telling you. I talked with her! I touched her!"

He pulled her closer and kissed her forehead. "Okay, we'll talk about it later. Let's just get you back to camp. The paramedics will want to check you out."

They climbed out of the forest and were greeted by the Yates', the Maynard's, and Ken Atwater. Matt escorted her to the office area where the paramedics took her into the ambulance. She found Rachel sitting holding an ice bag on the back of her head.

"Are you okay?" Rachel asked.

"I'm fine, Rach," she said and hugged Rachel tightly. "Trina said she killed you. I'm sorry for dragging you into this."

"You didn't drag me into it. Remember, I came willingly," Rachel said, rolling her eyes.

The paramedic removed the ice bag from Rachel's head for one last look before he applied a bandage. "Did you stop to help her before you ran off?" he asked Julie.

"No. Why?"

"When we found her we noticed some dark blue powder on her wound. Apparently it stopped the bleeding. I'm pretty sure that if that powder hadn't been there, Rachel here would have been in really bad shape."

Julie sighed. *Thank you, Victoria.*

She stopped short of telling Rachel about her visit with Victoria; she would wait for a time when they were alone. Both women emerged from the ambulance and Julie found Mike waiting for her.

"Honey, are you okay?" he asked, hugging her tightly. He brushed her hair back from her face.

"Yeah, I'm fine. Just a few scratches. I'll be alright," Julie said.

Matt walked over to them. "Trina's in custody. Jerry says he didn't know anything about it. We'll question him some more, just to be sure he's telling us the truth."

"Did she say anything?" Julie asked.

"Yeah, she wants her lawyer. What happened out here last night?"

"Stupid me, it's all my fault. I just couldn't wait for you to look for that package. I talked Rachel into going with me. We went over to the trailhead and were trying to find whatever it was I saw last night. Trina surprised me and she admitted to killing Willis. Then she said she killed that Dillon guy in Cleveland, too. She said it got easier the more she did it. That she did it for the money. Then she said she killed Rachel and that I was next. That's when I kicked her in the face and ran."

"So that's how she got that swollen cheek. I thought it came from the forest floor," Matt replied.

"Nope, t'was me. But how did you find out about Trina?"

"Like I said, Willis' computer. He played that geo treasure hunt game, too."

Julie looked at her brother. "That's what Trina said. She said he was always getting the prizes and that he was not gonna get the ten thousand bucks. That's when she stabbed him."

"Well, Willis' computer showed that he was doing the geo treasure hunting for the big bucks, but never input the winning code. The forensic investigation on his computer found that he sent messages to Trina and Jerry. I just got this feeling about them and Sarah and I hauled ass back here. I felt we had a suspect, or suspects. We just didn't know if they were both in on it. We came back here and went to their camper, but Jerry was the only one there. Couldn't imagine where Trina was."

He flashed a grin. "I came over to the bus and knocked on your door, but you, sister dear, were not home. Seems you and Rachel were out playing around in the woods. I called for backup and prayed that you had your hiker finders with you. We found Rachel and called for medical. That's when we knew you were out there somewhere. Your signal was real faint for a long time, and we couldn't get a fix on you, so we just went looking. But with no moon, it was pitch black. We literally stumbled across Trina. She had been knocked out and the knife was still in her hand. I thought the sun would never come up. Right about daybreak your signal got really strong. That's when we knew we had you. Thank God for the hiker finder."

"Matt, can I take her back to the bus?" Mike asked.

"Sure, why don't you three go back? I've got things to wrap up here. I'll be over later. I'll get breakfast in town, but let's cook out later tonight. I should be back in time for a good steak. How 'bout it, Mike? Red meat for all of us?"

"Sounds great! I'll run into town later and pick up some steaks at Harps. They always have big, honkin' ones."

"Ya know, as good as that sounds, I think I'll have a chicken breast." Julie added. "That and a salad will do just fine."

"Okay by me, hon. Whatever you want," Mike replied and kissed her.

The three walked slowly to the campsite. "That was crazy, wasn't it?" Rachel asked.

"Yeah, but not as crazy as my night in the forest."

"What do you mean?"

"I'll tell you later. How's your head?"

"It aches."

They sat at the picnic table; the morning sun began to peek over the tall oaks that surrounded the campground.

"You guys hungry? I'll make breakfast," Mike said.

"Yeah, I could use something," Julie replied.

"Me too," said Rachel.

Mike popped up and leaped into the bus. "Bacon and French toast for all."

Julie watched as Mike closed the front door, and then turned to Rachel. "I know you're not going to believe this, but my great-grandmother, Victoria, saved my life last night."

"Victoria? She was there? In the forest? That's impossible."

"Yeah, I know. Remember those two stone boobs by the tree? Her cabin was right there. Those stones are the grave markers of her parents. My great-great grandparents. She took me into her cabin and we talked all night about her life. I remember everything she said. It was wonderful."

Rachel looked at Julie. "Are you sure you weren't hallucinating? You know you were out in that forest all night. This sounds nuts."

"I know it sounds ridiculous, but I'm telling you, I held her hands. I hugged her. She was real. She told me she lives in the Spirit World and watches over me. And I'm pretty sure she saved your life, too."

Rachel stared at Julie in disbelief. "Me? How?"

"A little blue powder."

Rachel reached for the back of her head and felt the bandage. "Wow."

"I know, she put some on my knee, too," Julie said, teary-eyed.

Rachel looked down at Julie's knee and saw the powder residue. "Alright, say I believe you, sort of," Rachel said and looked up toward the sky. "Thank you, Victoria." Then she looked at Julie. "Maybe we should both take a nap after breakfast. I know I'm beat and you've got to be exhausted."

"Actually, I'm not that tired," Julie replied.

Mike emerged from the bus with a tray of French toast, bacon, butter and syrup, and the three ate breakfast at the picnic table. Even though it wasn't on her diet, Julie decided to forgive herself and indulge one last time.

After they finished breakfast, Julie yawned. "I think I'll take Rachel's advice and get some rest. Mike, honey, wake me up in a couple of hours, will you?"

"Sure, babe," Mike said and hugged her tightly. "I love you. I thought I'd lost you. I never want that to happen."

"I love you too, honey. Are you starting to grow a mustache?"

Mike smiled and kissed her. "Maybe."

"I like it."

She stepped into the bus and slowly walked back to the bedroom. She wasn't tired, but she ached, and a nap just sounded good. After popping a couple of ibuprofen, she sat on the edge of the bed and removed her shoes and socks. She wondered if the time she spent with Victoria was just a figment of her imagination. After all, it was pretty far fetched. Spirit World? Mysterious cabins?

"Whew, Victoria, that was quite a ride you gave me," she said softly.

She stood up and stripped off her shorts. Finally she pulled off her top, and looked in the mirror that hung on the closet door, hoping the scratches on her face wouldn't leave scars. *What's this?* A strip of leather hung around her neck; a cougar's claw dangled from it.

She slowly reached up and clutched the claw. "Victoria," she whispered. Fresh tears welled up. "I'll remember."

She climbed into bed still holding the cougar claw and relived the events of the night. *What a story. No one will ever believe me. But I know she's out there.* She closed her eyes.

As she began to drift off to sleep, she heard a voice softly whisper, "*Ne pas craindre quel est pour venir. L'embrasser, mon doux.* Do not fear what is to come. Embrace it.*"

Chapter 23

Linkford Cemetery
Near Graniteville, Missouri

"Here it is, Michael. Turn here."

Mike eased the car past the black wrought iron gate and onto the narrow white rock path that meandered through the old cemetery.

"Okay. Now where?" he asked.

"She said we would find them next to the twin oak trees. I imagine we're talking about two huge ones by now. Hopefully they're still standing."

By current standards, the Linkford Cemetery was small, about two acres in total area, established even before Graniteville was a town. Headstones here were old, some broken and difficult to read; the earliest ones dating back to 1805. Not many visitors came to Linkford Cemetery. Few remembered it even existed. But at least someone kept the grounds mowed – maybe a relative.

Julie spied several large oak trees at the back of one row.

"Maybe this is it."

They stepped out into an oppressive heat. Julie was right; it would be a hot summer. They each carried a bouquet of silk flowers.

"I'm glad these flowers are fake. They'd never make it," Mike said.

"Yeah, there's not a breath of air. Thank goodness for the trees." The old cemetery had one thing going for it – plenty of mature trees, their branches spread out like huge umbrellas and the leaves offered welcome shade to most of the area. Even so, both Julie and Mike were sweating as they made their way to the stand of oaks.

"I'll take the right side, you go left," Mike said.

Julie stepped cautiously, trying to avoid grave sites. *I hate walking through cemeteries. I always feel like I'm disturbing their sleep.* "Anything over there?" she called out to Mike.

"Not yet," Mike replied. "I sure hope we find them soon. I think the silk is melting."

She must have looked at twenty headstones and turned toward the back row when Mike shouted. "Hey, hon. I think I found 'em."

She hurried to Mike and found herself looking down at two plain, arched headstones located directly under massive twin oak trees...

Victoria Jochem	*Rogers Jochem*
1852-1936	1847-1897

"I finally found you, Victoria. And Dutch, too," Julie sighed.

"Well, I have to admit, babe. I didn't think we would find them, but you were right."

"Of course I was right. Victoria told me where to look."

"I know what you said about that night, Jules, but I just can't believe it."

"That's alright, hon," she replied. "I understand." *It's the Cherokee in me.*

She stood lost in memories of the night two weeks before when Victoria had saved her life. *I remember everything you said, great-grandmother. And I'm writing it all down.*

Mike put his hand on her shoulder and brought her back. "I think I understand why you wanted to find her, Jules."

"Why?"

"Well, it kinda like…completes the circle."

She reached up and kissed his cheek. "By jove, I think you're catching on, Watson. Maybe we'll work on your side now."

"Maybe." He cupped her face in his hand. "Ready?"

"Yeah," she said and knelt down and placed the bouquets on the graves.

"I brought you and great-grandpa something, Victoria. I hope you like them. I feel better knowing where you are." *Not that I have to be here. All I need to do is speak your name.*

Just then a soft, cool breeze washed gently over them.

"Man, that felt good," Mike said. "Where in the world did that come from?"

Julie looked up at him. "I think I know."

"You do?"

She gazed back at her great-grandmother's headstone and smiled. "Yeah, I do."

THE END

I had plenty of help on my first project.

Good friend Rick Hinds – retired sergeant from the Springfield, Illinois Police Department. Without him this project would never have been completed.

Long time friend, John Diefenback – retired Sangamon County Illinois Sheriff's deputy who also helped with police procedures.

Computer forensics guru and friend, Shawn Patrick.

Mr. Brick Autry of the Fort Davidson State Historic Site in Pilot Knob, Missouri.

Canadian friend, Margo Desjardins.

Cousins Barbara Dickson and Vicki Ridle for cemetery-hopping with me.

The manuscript department at the Abraham Lincoln Presidential Library in Springfield, Illinois.

The staff at the Athens Library Genealogy Section in Athens, Illinois.

Dear friends John Kennedy and Diane Carlson for their editing assistance.

My niece and editor, Tanya Little, who challenged me to become a more complete writer, and offered her ideas and support. Your Great-great grandmother must have been talking to you, too.

About the author

Laetitia "Tish" Cook was born and raised in Springfield, Illinois. She attended local schools, and after graduating from high school in 1967, began her career at Illinois Bell Telephone. She held various positions, and in 1978 was promoted to course developer/instructor, where she continued to write and deliver training until her retirement in 1998.

After discovering details of her great-grandmother's life, she decided to put it in print and wrote her first fiction novel, *When You Speak My Name*.

Tish lives just outside of Springfield with her husband, John and family pets Max and Rudy.